Usborne
Illustrated
Myths
from Around
the World

Usborne
Illustrated
Myths
from Around
the World

Illustrated by Anja Klauss

Contents

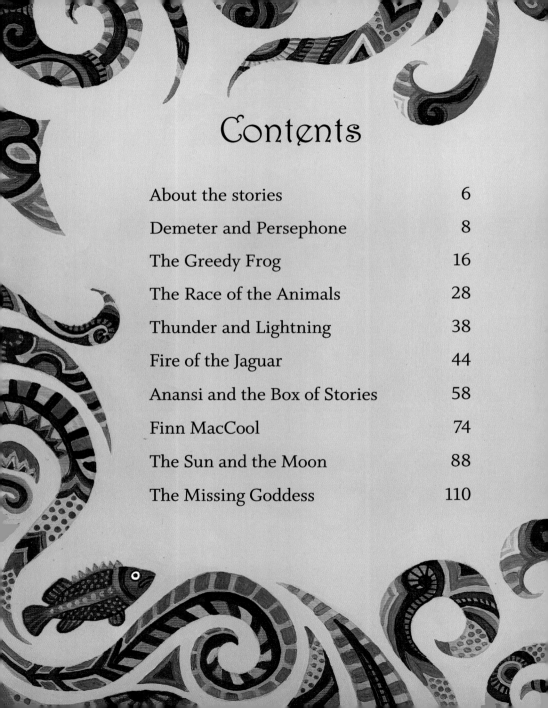

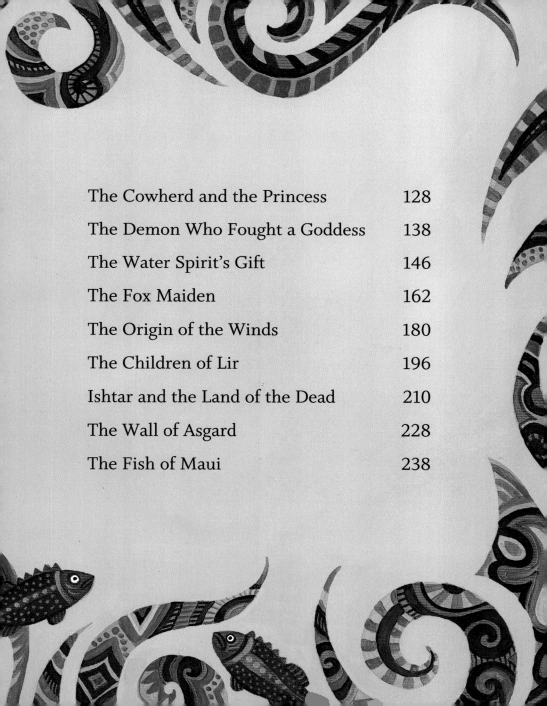

About the stories

Long ago, everything from the changing of the seasons to the passage of the Sun through the sky was an unsolved mystery. So people came up with stories to explain how things came to be. These stories – known as myths or fables – varied from place to place, but all had a shared thread running through them: they set out to explain the inexplicable, to offer a version of the world that made sense.

The stories in this book are hundreds or thousands of years old. They were first being told long before the advent of science, when people still

commonly believed in giants and spirits and mythical beings, that could change from one form to another in the blink of an eye. Between these pages you'll meet a spider who can outwit a god, a frog who drains the world of water, fierce goddesses, trickster gods and a doll who unleashes the winds.

After so much time and so many tellings, these stories may no longer be quite the same tales – or have quite the same meanings – as when they were first told. But that doesn't make them any less exciting. Read on to discover eighteen wonderful myths and fables from around the world...

In ancient Greece, Demeter was worshipped
as goddess of the harvest and agriculture.
This story, of her love and loss, explains how
the seasons came to be.

Demeter and Persephone

At the beginning of the world, there were no seasons. All year round, the rain fell and the sun shone, crops grew and fruit dropped ripe and luscious from the trees. Flowers blossomed in the meadows and new shoots sprang from the fertile soil.

Tending them all was Demeter, goddess of the harvest. At her side, as fair as the wildflowers, was her daughter, Persephone, beloved by all and adored by her mother.

But another god had his eye on her... Hades, lord of the underworld, had spied Persephone and wanted her for himself. He went to Zeus, king of the gods, to seek permission, and to his delight, Zeus agreed to his plan. As long as he could snatch her away, Persephone would be his.

Hades watched and he waited until Persephone was out alone one day in a field of golden corn. As she walked among their shining stems, she felt the ground tremble beneath her feet. With a great crack, the Earth opened before her, revealing a dark chasm.

And out of it, on a horse-drawn chariot of black and gold, swept Hades.

He plucked Persephone from the field, as easily as if she were a flower herself, and then swept her down, down, down into the underworld. The chasm closed over their heads and all was quiet. All was dark...

When Demeter discovered her daughter was missing, she was inconsolable. She began to search the world for her, neglecting the Earth she so loved. Flowers died, crops withered, fruit failed to ripen and the soil turned to chalky dust. People and animals starved, but Demeter didn't notice.

At last, Helios, the sun god, took pity on her. "Demeter," he said, "I saw on my travels what happened. Hades, god of the underworld, has snatched your daughter away."

"So she's in the Land of the Dead!" wailed Demeter. "How has Zeus let this happen?"

"Zeus knew all along..." confessed Helios.

In a fury, Demeter stormed Zeus' palace on Mount Olympus. "How could you let my daughter be taken from me?" she raged.

Zeus looked down at the withered Earth, the starving people and the dying plants, and admitted something had to be done. So he called for Hermes, the winged messenger, and sent him down to the underworld. "Bring back Persephone," he commanded, "or all is lost."

Down in the darkness of the underworld, Persephone missed the sunlight and the warmth and the flowers of the world above, but most of all she missed her mother.

Hades, however, treated her with kindliness and gentleness. She was intrigued by the dark caverns of this new realm, its glittering gemstones and the piteous plight of the souls of the dead. Could she, after all, become queen of the underworld?

Hades sat beside her, day after day, urging her to be happy, tempting her to eat.

"Just a few tiny mouthfuls," he coaxed, tipping some pomegranate seeds into the palm of her hand. "Come Persephone. Taste them! They're like glinting jewels."

Tentatively, Persephone looked down at the juicy red seeds. Then she popped one, two, three, four, five, six into her mouth. Hades watched her eat each one with glowing satisfaction.

Then came a rushing of wind, like the sound of birds in flight, and the messenger Hermes stood before them.

"Ah, a visitor," said Hades. "I've been expecting you."

"I come from Zeus," replied Hermes. "Hades, you must let Persephone return. The king of the gods demands it."

"Of course I obey Zeus in all things," said Hades. "But in this, I can't!" He held up his hands in mock sorrow. "There is a law, is there not, that it is only possible to leave the underworld if no food has passed your lips?"

"That is so," said Hermes.

Persephone gasped. "Yes, my love," said Hades. "You have just eaten six seeds..."

Hermes paused. There was a deal to be done here, and he loved nothing more than a deal. If he returned without

Persephone, Zeus would never forgive him and the Earth would suffer. But nor could he break the law the Fates had made at the dawn of time.

"Six seeds shall equal six months," said Hermes. "For six months of the year, Persephone shall live down here in the darkness, with Hades, as queen of the underworld. For the other six she may return to Earth, and tend to the flowers and the fruit and the soil with her mother."

Persephone smiled. "It is a fair plan," she said.

And so, for six months of the year, when Persephone reigned in darkness, Demeter wept. The leaves fell from the trees, the land was whipped by cold wind and her tears fell as rain. Then in spring, when Persephone returned, the Earth burst into life with Demeter's joy. New shoots appeared, flowers blossomed and crops ripened under a golden sun. So it went, year after year, cycle after cycle.

And this is how the seasons came to be.

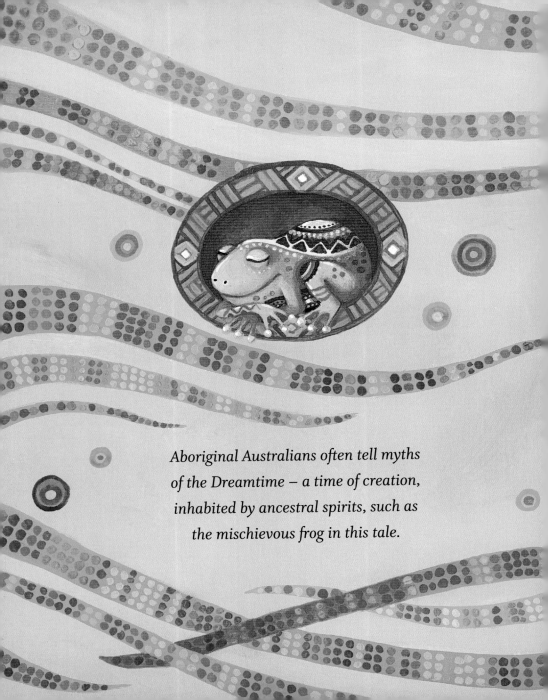

Aboriginal Australians often tell myths
of the Dreamtime – a time of creation,
inhabited by ancestral spirits, such as
the mischievous frog in this tale.

The Greedy Frog

Tiddalik the frog was fast asleep. He had been sleeping for years, curled up in a ball underground. None of the other animals knew where he was, or even if he was still alive.

17

It was only when a powerful storm arrived, filling the sky with booming thunder and pelting the ground with stinging rain that Tiddalik finally woke up.

Slowly – very slowly – he opened one eye. Then, just as slowly, he opened the other. With a grunt and a sigh he began to dig his way to the surface.

"At last," he gasped, when his head popped out of the soggy soil. With one final kick of his back legs, he hopped right out of the ground, landing with a *splat* in front of a rather shocked platypus. "Wh... who are you?" the platypus stammered, unsure of what to make of this sudden, surprising creature.

Tiddalik yawned. "Who am I? What are you talking about? It's me, Tiddalik. Don't you recognize me?"

"Tiddalik?" replied the platypus, squinting as he tried to identify the frog under all the mud. "Where have you been hiding all of these years?"

For a second, the frog looked confused. "Has it really been years?" he murmured. He shook his head. "There was a terrible drought, so I decided to burrow underground and take a little nap, until the water returned. I suppose I must have overslept..."

The platypus was incredulous. "You were asleep this whole time? No wonder I didn't recognize you. And you're so thin! Come, follow me, there's a lake nearby. You must be really thirsty."

Tiddalik followed the platypus to an enormous lake, bustling with all kinds of animals. Ducks and geese swam across its surface. Herons waded in the shallows, hunting water spiders. Even a crocodile was sprawled out on a far bank, basking in the sun after the storm.

The moment Tiddalik saw the shimmering water, his eyes lit up. He had been dreaming about water for years, but he had forgotten how beautiful it could be. He raced to the edge of the lake and took a few delicious sips.

The platypus smiled. "I knew you were thirsty," he said, smugly. But he didn't know just how thirsty.

What started off as a few small sips quickly became massive gulps. "More!" Tiddalik gurgled, unable to satisfy his thirst. He swallowed more and more water, growing larger and larger while the lake began to shrink.

"Stop – that's enough!" cried the platypus, watching in horror as Tiddalik gulped down the lake. But instead of stopping, the frog opened his mouth even wider.

Glug! The herons found themselves plodding through mud. *Glug!* The ducks and geese had to fly away to avoid being swallowed. *Glug!* Fish of all shapes and sizes were suddenly flapping about on dry land.

The Greedy Frog

When at last the lake was completely drained dry,
Tiddalik was so big and bloated he could barely breathe. The
other animals looked at him with a mixture of fear and
anger. Only the crocodile, seemingly unconcerned by the
frog's greed, continued to laze in the sun.

"Look at what you did," yelled the platypus. "Give us
back our water!"

But Tiddalik was not done. "So thirsty..." he croaked,
looking around for more. In the distance he spotted a long,
winding river, sparkling as it snaked across the plain.
Without a moment's hesitation he set off for it, bouncing
and rolling all the way. The animals chased after him,
shouting as they went.

When Tiddalik reached the river, he opened his mouth
wider than ever before and began slurping up the water
from the river. This time, his gulps were so powerful, they
sucked in water from all across the land. With each
mouthful, a lake shrank or a stream dwindled until they

were devoured altogether by the thirsty frog. When he was done, not even a puddle remained. Tiddalik was now bigger than a hill, and still he wasn't happy. "I want more!" he said.

"There *is* no more!" the platypus called from below. "You've taken it all – and it's time you gave it back."

Tiddalik scoffed. "Why should I? If you wanted this water so badly, maybe you should have drunk it first. But you didn't. Now leave me alone." The frog let out a massive yawn. "I want another nap."

"Oh no you don't," the platypus shouted. "You give us back our water right now... or else."

On hearing the platypus' threat, Tiddalik began to smile. Compared to Tiddalik, the platypus was tiny. What could a tiny platypus do to a giant frog? The thought was enough to make him laugh. But the moment he did, his belly tightened, causing a fountain of water to erupt from his mouth. At once, the frog clamped his mouth shut, refusing to let out any more.

"Aha!" said the platypus, watching water trickle down the frog's chin onto his swollen belly. "Now I know just how to get our water back."

He turned to the others and began whispering his plan. When he was done, the spiny echidna took a step forward.

"Give us back our water, you greedy frog!" she squeaked. But the frog just snorted and rolled his eyes. "So be it," she said, and rolled up into a ball.

Tiddalik smirked. "You won't be able to pop me with your sharp spines," he said, matter-of-factly.

But instead, the echidna rolled on to her back and then unfolded into the most bizarre pose. Her long tongue was lolling out of her mouth, her legs were stretched wide in all directions, and she was singing a song in the silliest voice.

At first, the frog thought the echidna was crazy. Then he spotted an owl twirling around and around on his feet until he was so dizzy, he fell over. Alongside him was a koala, juggling mice so badly that most of the time they landed on her face and had to run down her shoulders and along her arms, back into her hands in order to be juggled again. The frog suppressed a giggle. It was all so ridiculous.

Tiddalik watched as the platypus started quacking like a duck, and a duck started growling like a tiger quoll. Even the lazy crocodile was dancing upright on his back legs. The frog felt his stomach groan and clamped his mouth tight shut. Beads of sweat were running down his face as he struggled not to laugh.

Then came the eel. She stood up on her tail and began waggling to and fro, tying herself in a series of knots. By mistake, she wove herself into such a tight knot that she couldn't get out of it again.

She wriggled around on the floor, calling for help. That was far more than Tiddalik could cope with. His belly let out a great grumbling sound, louder than thunder, and a torrent of water exploded from his mouth. He roared with laughter – hard enough that he thought he might split in two – spewing out more and more water with each guffaw. At first, the animals cheered, but their joy turned to panic when the water started rising around them.

"What do we do?" the echidna cried.

The platypus hadn't thought that far ahead. He had just assumed all the water would go back to where it had come from. Instead, it was pouring out of the frog in every direction, making new rivers wherever it fell. "There's only one thing we can do–" shouted the platypus, "–run away!"

As quickly as they could, the animals ran, flew, hopped and slithered away in search of dry land until only Tiddalik was left. With an ear-popping burp, a final stream gushed from the frog's mouth – along with a rather confused catfish.

"Well, that was rather unpleasant," said the fish, before swimming away.

"Yes," agreed Tiddalik, small again, and even thinner than before. He felt sick to his stomach and more than a little sorry for himself. "I don't think I'll be doing that again."

In China, the years are named after twelve animals
– each of which can be seen as a pattern of stars in the
night sky. This is the story of how they decided which
year would be named after which animal.

The Race of the Animals

It was almost the start of the Chinese New Year. But instead of preparing to celebrate, as people do now, with feasting and fireworks, everyone was covering their ears and cowering, trying to block out the sounds of a terrible argument...

It had all started with the rat. "What shall we *call* the new year?" it squeaked, sitting up and snuffling its sharp pink nose. "It needs a name!"

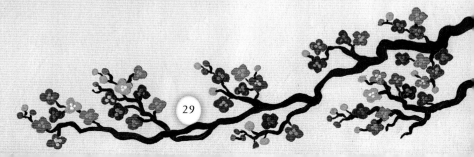

The other animals answered eagerly and all at once.

"Let's call it... the year of the ox!" bellowed the big brown ox.

"Baaaaah, no," bleated the curly-horned ram. "The year of the ram!"

"Monkey, monkey, monkey," chattered the mischievous monkey. "The year of the monkey!"

"I say, the year of the dog!" yapped the dog, bouncing up and down on all four paws.

"Rrrrr-ridiculous," rumbled the tiger, frowning. "The year of the tiger sounds much better!"

"But not as good as the year of the rooster!" squawked the rooster, fluffing out his feathers. "Cock-a-doodle-doo!"

"Hmmm," yawned the dragon, as steam billowed from his jaws. "I prefer the year of the dragon!"

"Why not pig?" grunted the pig lazily.

"Or horse," snorted the horse, pawing at the ground impatiently.

"Ssssurely you mean ssss-snake?" hissed the snake.

"Or rabbit, perhaps?" put in the rabbit timidly.

"But I'm the strongest!" boomed the ox.

"I'm the cleverest," screeched the monkey.

"I'm better looking!" crowed the rooster.

"But it was MY idea," squealed the rat.

Their squeaking and squawking and snapping and snorting grew louder and louder, until...

"QUIET!" rang out a stern voice. The gods had come down from heaven to see what was the matter. "Why are you making this dreadful noise?"

So the animals explained that each beast wanted to name the coming year after itself. "How can we decide between us?" they asked.

The gods thought for a moment. Then one of them pointed to a wide expanse of silvery water which flowed nearby.

"Why not have a race?" he said. "Look at that river. We will name the new year after whichever animal is first to reach the other side."

The animals looked. They were all good swimmers, and the river rippled invitingly in the sunshine.

"Very well," they squeaked and squawked and growled. "We will race and name the new year after the winner. But what about the rest of us?"

"Whoever comes second, shall give his name to the second year, whoever is third, to the third year – and so on..." answered the god. He tallied up the animals. "There are twelve of you in all, so we shall name twelve years."

The animals nodded, satisfied. Eagerly, they lined up on the shore.

"One, two, three... GO!"

Splish – splash – SPLOSH! Twelve animals plunged into the cool water and began swimming as hard as they could. The smaller animals paddled furiously, churning the surface into a foaming froth, while the bigger animals moved slowly but strongly. Tiger cut through the waves with gleaming claws. Dragon swept along elegantly, scales shining in the wet. But it was huge, hefty Ox who pulled steadily into the lead...

Rat scrabbled desperately with his little pink paws, but it was no use – Ox was about to overtake.

"I'll never win like this," Rat thought to himself. "I'd better do something, quick!"

As Ox's tail trailed past in the shimmering water, Rat grabbed hold of it. Then he climbed up it, right onto Ox's broad, brown back.

Ox didn't pause. "It must be the water weeds tickling me," he thought, and kept on swimming. He didn't want to

waste even a moment looking around.

Softly, stealthily, Rat crept along Ox's back and onto his head, where he perched between the horns, grinning. "This is the best way to race," he chuckled to himself.

Soon, Ox was far ahead of the other animals. He swam and swam, his legs pulling powerfully through the clear, cool water.

"I'm going to win," he thought triumphantly, seeing the empty riverbank ahead. Just before he reached it, however, Rat gave a mighty leap – and landed on the bank just in front of Ox's astonished nose.

"I win!" called Rat, doing a little jig.

"Where did you come from?" spluttered Ox, gaping.

"The top of your head," giggled Rat.

"You cheat!" roared Ox. He heaved himself out of the river, water sloshing, and stamped his hooves in fury. "What do the gods say?"

"We say that you are very strong, Ox, and Rat is very

clever," they answered. "So, we will call the first year, the year of the rat –" Ox snorted loudly – "and the second year shall be the year of the ox. Well done to you both."

The next animal to wade ashore, showering the bank in crystal drops, was Tiger – so the third year became the year of the tiger. Rabbit and Dragon followed shortly after – so the fourth year became the year of the rabbit, and the fifth became the year of the dragon. And so it went on, with the snake, the horse, the ram, the monkey, the rooster and the dog – who shook water all over everyone else, much to their annoyance.

Last to finish was Pig, puffing and blowing and rather pink from the effort. So the twelfth and final year became the year of the pig.

"Last but not least," as Pig likes to say to his friends.

And that is the story of the great race of the animals, and how they named the years.

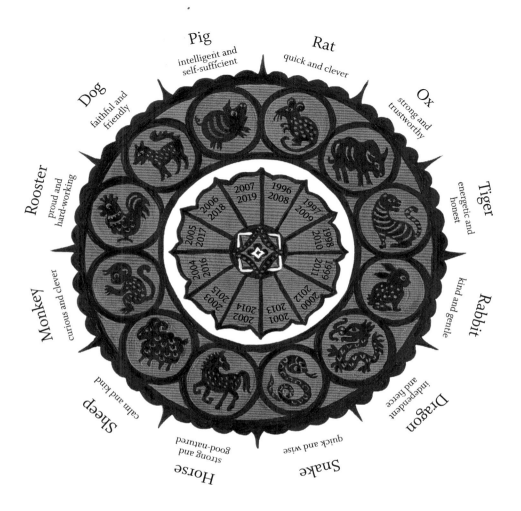

Here are the twelve animals, arranged in order.
People born in the year of a certain animal are
thought to share some of its character traits.

This ancient tale comes from the west coast of Africa — one of many myths that tell how something came to be.

Thunder and Lightning

They say in Africa that Thunder and Lightning
once lived on the Earth, not up in the sky as they
do today. Thunder was an old mother sheep, with a coat
as black as storm clouds and a loud, rumbling voice,
while Lightning, her son, was a fiery golden ram.

✿ Thunder and Lightning ✿

To begin with, the two of them lived right alongside people. Some of the time, this was a good thing for everyone. When the fields grew too dry, they would invite their friend, Rain, to visit from the coast. Rain would frisk over the hills, heavy drops falling from his curly coat and spattering the dusty ground, bringing forth green shoots.

Sometimes, though, they were dangerous. Lightning had a hot temper and when he grew angry, he spat blazing firebolts at anyone and anything that annoyed him...

Kaboom! A tree became a blackened stump. Kablam! A straw hut burned to the ground. Kazam! A field was ablaze.

Each time, Thunder would shout at him. "STOP! STOP!" Her ear-splitting rebukes rumbled across the plains.

But it was no good. Things still got fizzled and frazzled and fried... until at last, the people had had enough. Their chief went to see the loud-mouthed mother and her hot-headed son.

"Thunder and Lightning, this is too dangerous," he told them. "You cannot live so close to us. You must move to the hills."

So Thunder and Lightning went to live among the steep slopes and rocky summits of the highest hills. But Lightning was still trouble. Now when Rain came to visit, Lightning wanted to play chase at breakneck speed across the hilltops.

"Slow down," Thunder would roar, so loudly that

people for miles around would cower and cover their ears. Only now, her voice boomed and echoed around the hills so that no one could make out the words.

And, although they were further away, there were still accidents. Lightning was just too hot-headed and too strong. His energy crackled through the air and if he ever lost his temper...

Kazam! A carefully planted crop became smoking stubble. Kazoom! A haystack burned to a crisp. Kablam! A logpile turned to cinders.

"Stop it!" Thunder would yell – but Lightning couldn't or wouldn't listen. So things still got charred and scorched and seared... until eventually, the chief told Thunder and Lightning that they would have to move further still.

"No one on Earth is safe with you here," he insisted. "You'll have to go and live in the sky!"

So today, Lightning romps around among the clouds high overhead, while old Thunder watches over him. If

Lightning gets carried away, his bright fizzing bolts slice through empty air, usually harmlessly. But sometimes they fall to Earth, burning whatever they touch – and then you will hear Thunder's booming voice telling him to be more careful.

This myth was first told by the Kayapo
people of Brazil, whose stories are filled
with the fantastic plants and animals of
the Amazon rainforest.

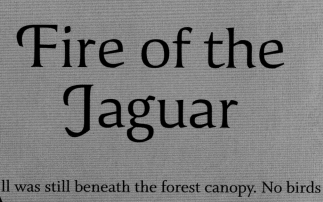

Fire of the Jaguar

All was still beneath the forest canopy. No birds soared, no beasts climbed or crawled. The only movement was the rustling of palm leaves up above, stirred by the gentlest of breezes.

"GO, Botoque!" came a sudden shout.

Instantly, two boys erupted from the undergrowth, shrieking loudly and startling a pair of bright red macaws from their nest. The boys took aim, drew back their arms and, a moment later, their spears whistled through the air, narrowly missing the scarlet birds.

"You were too slow, Botoque," muttered the oldest boy, skulking ahead to collect his fallen spear. "Now what will we take back to the village for dinner?"

The boys had been hunting all day, and so far they had nothing to show for it. If they were to return home empty-handed, their family would go to bed hungry.

Botoque scratched his head. "The birds are gone. But their nest is still here, up in that kapok tree," he said, pointing at a small hollow, high up in the tree. "I bet they left their eggs behind – we could bring those back."

The older boy looked up to where Botoque pointed. "Don't be a fool! You can't climb up there. However do you expect to get back down?"

But before he could finish, Botoque had started to climb the huge tree, slowly but surely making his way up to the nest. When he got there, he called down to his brother: "Two! There are two eggs here!"

Botoque's brother sighed. "Well then, throw them down!" And he held out his hands, ready to catch them.

Botoque carefully lifted out the eggs, lined them up above his brother, and dropped them.

The moment the eggs landed in the older boy's outstretched hands, he let out an almighty yell. "OUCH! Botoque! What are you doing, dropping stones on me?"

"What are you talking about?" said Botoque, confused. "I dropped the eggs as you asked me to."

Botoque's brother lifted his hands to the sky. "If they were eggs you dropped, do you think I would have hurt my hands like this? No, you dropped two huge stones."

"I... I... I don't understand," babbled Botoque, looking

back and forth between the nest and his brother. "I was sure they were eggs!"

But Botoque's brother had had enough. "I'm going home," he shouted. "You can find your own way back." And he stormed off, taking both spears with him.

"Brother, wait! I'm stuck!" cried Botoque, gingerly moving along a branch, trying to work out how to make his way back down. But his older brother was long gone.

Hours passed when, at last, Botoque heard the crunching of twigs and the shifting of leaves beneath him. His heart leaped in his chest. "Brother has forgiven me," he whispered to himself. "He's come to rescue me!"

Botoque's excitement quickly disappeared when a strange laugh echoed among the trees – as wild as the roar of a great predator, but light-hearted, like the chuckle of a full-grown man. As Botoque looked on, a jaguar stepped out into the open, standing on two feet, with a bow in one hand, and an arrow in the other.

Up until this point, Botoque had never seen a bow and arrow before. He had also never seen a jaguar, on two *or* four feet.

"What are you?" he called out, his eyes wide with fear.

"Me?" snorted the jaguar. "Why, I'm Jaguar, of course. And I know *exactly* what you are." He licked his lips, then smiled a wicked, toothy grin.

"Wh...what am I?" asked Botoque.

"You're *stuck*," said Jaguar, almost purring in amusement. "I thought that was pretty obvious. You humans are such funny creatures, always getting yourselves into the strangest situations."

Carefully, Jaguar slid the bow and arrow into a quiver on his back. He bent low to the ground, then sprang forward, darting up and along the trunk to where Botoque was stranded. Before Botoque could act, Jaguar grabbed him by the waist and pulled him free from the tree.

"Aaah!" cried Botoque, finding his voice in time to scream as he and Jaguar hurtled to the ground, where they landed with a soft thud on the forest floor.

"Calm down, human," said Jaguar. "You're safe now."

But Botoque would not calm down. The moment he was on his feet, he was backing away from Jaguar, his fists up, ready to fight. Then he caught a whiff of something delicious. He sniffed once, sniffed twice, before spotting the basket of fresh meat hanging alongside Jaguar's bow. His belly let out an enormous growl.

Jaguar laughed, wilder than ever. "Your stomach could teach me a thing or two about growling," he said with a smile. "Now come along, boy. I will prepare you some food, and you will see that I am no enemy."

Jaguar stalked off through the forest and a few minutes

later, a cautious but curious Botoque followed behind him, hugging his rumbling belly as he went.

"Please do come in," said Jaguar when they arrived at his home. "Warm yourself by the fire and tell me stories of your village while I cook us some meat."

"Cook?" asked Botoque. Then, "Fire?"

Botoque had never heard of such things. So the moment he entered Jaguar's musty home and saw a bright, hot *something* dancing and flickering across a pile of logs, all he could do was gasp.

"What is *that?*" asked Botoque, afraid to take another step inside.

"That? Why, that's fire," Jaguar grinned. "There's no need to be afraid. I will teach you all about it."

And that's just what Jaguar did. Over the next few days, he taught Botoque about the uses of fire. He showed him how to cook meat, making it taste sublime. He explained how fire could warm you on a cold day, and how dangerous

it was if you did not treat it with respect. And when he was done, he taught Botoque how to use a bow and arrow, too.

"Now that I have shared the secrets of fire with you," said Jaguar, after a week had passed, "you must promise never to share it with humankind."

Botoque was taken aback. How could he keep the wonders of fire from his people? He started to complain, but a low growl from Jaguar made him change his mind. "I promise," he said, a little glumly.

Jaguar smiled, and from then on, Botoque was his valued guest, often visiting from his village to eat cooked meat and tell tales of his life. All was peaceful, until the day Jaguar's wife returned home after many weeks away, exhausted from her travels...

"Who is this in my house?" she snarled, dropping a huge basket of meat, letting its contents spill across the floor.

Jaguar had left to gather more wood for the fire, and Botoque was all alone, his mouth stuffed full of food.

Before Botoque had a chance to swallow, let alone explain what he was doing there, Jaguar's wife charged at him. In a fury, she swiped at him with her needle-sharp claws, almost raking his chest. "Thief! Villain! Get out of my home!" she shrieked.

In a rush of fear, Botoque sped from Jaguar's house, knocking his angry wife aside as he fled. He could hear her yelling behind him as he darted between trees and ducked beneath branches. He looked back only once, in time to see Jaguar's wife aiming an arrow at his back.

Thankfully for Botoque, by the time she let it fly, he was too far away, and the arrow skidded harmlessly to a halt across a mossy log.

Back at the village, Botoque's family surrounded him with concern. He looked a mess. His hair was matted with twigs and leaves, and his breathing was frantic. "What's wrong?" they asked. "What happened to you?"

Forgetting his promise to Jaguar, Botoque explained everything that had happened to him from the moment he had scaled the kapok tree. He told them about fire and cooked meat and bows and arrows. He told them about Jaguar and his wife – and where they lived.

"How dare they attack you, a guest in their home!" said Botoque's father, outraged. "Clearly they do not deserve the wonders they've kept hidden from us."

By this time, Botoque had recovered enough from his shock to see the wrong he had done, breaking his promise to Jaguar. "They're not evil," Botoque protested. "It was simply a mistake, I'm sure it was."

But it was too late. Nobody was listening to him. Their

hearts were too filled with rage, and their minds too clouded by imaginary fires and sizzling meat.

That night, Botoque's family dragged him into the forest, demanding he show them where Jaguar lived. Reluctantly, Botoque led them back to the kapok tree and, from there, to Jaguar's home.

When they arrived, they were delighted to discover that Jaguar and his wife were out on an evening prowl. They were even more delighted by the strange wonders that awaited them inside.

"It's so bright!" said Botoque's brother, squinting as he approached Jaguar's fire. Timidly, he reached out a hand to grab it, felt its intense heat prickling his fingers and quickly snapped it back.

"You shouldn't touch fire," said Botoque, knowingly. "Instead, grab a log and carry the fire upon it."

So Botoque's family each took a log and one by one carried away Jaguar's fire. But that was not all they took.

They also took Jaguar's cooked meat, along with his bow and arrows.

When Jaguar returned home, he found it a dark and empty place, his fire gone, his bow and arrows missing.

He fell to all fours and snarled at the sky – a terrifying sound filled with great anger and sadness, without any trace of laughter.

And that is why today Jaguar hunts without a bow, and why he eats his meat uncooked, and why he has no love of humans. All because, a long, long time ago, a boy broke his promise.

Anansi stories are 'trickster' folktales from
the Ashanti and the Akan people in Ghana.
From there, the stories spread through
West Africa and to the Caribbean.

Anansi and the Box of Stories

Anansi the spider was a trickster. Cunning and crafty, he could weave with words as well as with webs, so when he looked at the world he knew that something was missing... stories.

Not the stories *he* spun, full of fantastic lies and clever deceits, but stories to be told around a fire to ward off the darkness at night. Stories to spark the imagination and breathe life into the unknown; to be told to children before they fell asleep, and then to be passed on from father to son and mother to daughter and on and on and on...

And where were all these stories? Anansi knew full well where they were – with Nyame, the Sky God, locked in a wooden box. But would Nyame give the box to people? Never! He guarded it like a hawk and never let it far from his reach. Many had tried before and all had failed. If Anansi were to win over that brimming box of stories, he was going to have to use all of his cunning. He couldn't wait.

Anansi began to spin a great long thread – as long and strong as the rivers that roared through the forest. He made it reach all the way to the sky and then on eight grasping legs he scampered up it, up and up until he reached the heavens.

"Oh Nyame," said Anansi, bowing low before the Sky

God. "I have come for the box of
stories. Would you be so gracious
as to give it to me?"

Nyame's whole body
rocked with laughter. "Oh
Anansi," he mocked. "Only
you would be bold and brave
enough to ask for it. But my
answer, of course, is 'NO!'"

"But you must have a price,"
replied Anansi. "Everyone has a
price. What is yours?"

Nyame was silent for a while, delighting in thinking up
impossible requests that were sure to defeat the spider.
"Ooh! That's a good one," he thought. And then, "Oh yes!
This is even better!"

"Are you absolutely sure you want to know my price?"
asked Nyame.

"I'm sure," said Anansi.

"Many have tried," warned Nyame. "All have failed. These are hard tasks for a little spider."

Anansi was not so easily scared. "Name your price," he insisted.

"Very well," said Nyame. "Bring me Onini, the python, Osebo, the leopard and Mboro, the hive of hornets. And, let me see, one more I think. Ah, yes! Mmoatia. Then, and only then, will the box be yours."

"M-m-m-moatia?" stuttered Anansi, his eight legs trembling.

In all of Africa, everyone feared Onini, who could squeeze the life from a crocodile. People dreaded meeting Osebo, whose claws were sharper than knives and Mboro, whose stings burned hotter than the sun. But no one was feared more than Mmoatia... the invisible, bad-tempered spirit of the forest.

"But I'll do it," Anansi swore. "I can succeed where

others fail. I can be the one to unlock the box of stories."

So Anansi slid back down the thread, all the way down to Earth, plotting and planning as he went.

First, he decided, it was the turn of Onini, the python...

Early the next morning, Anansi headed for the forest, a long stick clutched in his claws. He scuttled under the biggest tree of them all and beneath its swaying branches he began to talk to himself. "I know I'm right," he muttered. "I know I am. He is much longer than this stick. Why will no one believe me?"

A long, lithe body uncoiled itself from the branch above and slithered down until it was head-high with Anansi.

"Sssssss," said Onini, the python. "What issss thissss you are talking about, Ananssssi? And you have woken me from my sssssslumbersss. How dare you!"

"Onini, I am so sorry," grovelled Anansi. "I didn't see you there. I have been telling everyone how long you are, how you are the longest and greatest snake in the forest. I've said

you are even longer than this huge stick, but not a single animal will believe me."

"Foolsssss!" said the snake. "Thissss issss easssily sssssorted. Let me lay myself out along the ground. Then I will prove that I am the greatest. I'll make this ssstick look like nothing more than a twig besssside me."

Then the great Onini slid down from the tree and stretched himself out alongside the stick. Anansi worked like lightning, darting this way and that, spinning his silken thread around the python until he was trapped fast against the stick.

"What trick isss thisss?" hissed Onini angrily, trying to thrash his body free from the thread. But nothing could break Anansi's web.

"Ha!" said Anansi. "Now come with me."

And he carried Onini up into the sky and presented him, with a flourish, to Nyame.

The Sky God looked on haughtily. "I'm not worried, little spider," he declared. "You still have the leopard and the hornets to catch. And of course, Mmoatia."

Anansi spun himself down from the sky and spent the day wrapped in thought. He had captured Onini by playing on his pride. Surely he could do the same with Osebo, the leopard?

The next day, Anansi waltzed over to where the sleek leopard was sunning himself on a large, flat rock. Anansi had a sack slung over his shoulder and, yet again, he was talking to himself.

"Leopard will never manage it. I told them once, I told them twice, he could never, ever do it, but would they believe me? No they would not..."

"What's this, Anansi?" said Osebo, yawning and stretching himself out to his full length.

Anansi caught a glimpse of Osebo's long, knife-like

claws, unsheathed and glinting in the sun. They would cut him in two in a moment, he knew, but he bravely carried on.

"I was talking to the other animals in the forest. I was saying how clever and cunning you are, but how even you couldn't squeeze yourself into this sack. But everyone else seemed to think you could."

"Ha!" said Osebo. "Let me prove you wrong. Hold open that sack and I'll be inside in the blink of an eye."

Suppressing his smile, Anansi held open the sack. Osebo leaped inside and Anansi bound it shut with his silken threads.

Osebo kicked and clawed and squirmed but there was nothing he could do to break free from the sack.

"You trickster!" Osebo cried. "I should have known better than to trust a spider."

"So you should," said Anansi. "But it's too late now." And once again he strung his threads up to the sky and presented Osebo to the Sky God.

"Two more to go," said Nyame. "That box of stories is still far from being yours..."

And Anansi knew it. Now he had to trap a hive of stinging hornets and carry them up to the sky. How was he going to do that?

After two nights of plotting and planning, Anansi could be found with a large gourd, full of water, and a plantain leaf, standing beneath the hornets' hive. They were buzzing furiously. Anansi thought for a moment of their poker-hot stings and then he thought of the box of stories, brimming with unspoken words.

He scuttled up the branch above the hornets' nest and poured the water from the gourd ALL OVER IT. Then he scuttled down again, a dripping plantain leaf perched upon his head.

"What's this?" cried the hornets angrily. "It's not the rainy season. Where has this water come from?"

"Oh Mboro," said Anansi. "I thought you would not be prepared for this sudden downpour. Look, I have come with a gourd so that you may take shelter inside it."

"Thank you," said the hornets. And they buzzed out of their hive and into the gourd.

As soon as the last one had passed through the opening, Anansi placed the plantain leaf over the hole and bound it on with his strongest silk. Then he went up to the Sky God, the gourd thrumming angrily with a mass of furious hornets.

"Hmm," said Nyame. "And *still* I'm not worried. For as we all know, Mmoatia will be the hardest of all to catch."

Anansi did know this. And he spent many

days and nights pondering the problem. How to trap something he couldn't even see?

At last, he came up with a plan. He carved a little wooden doll and covered it with sticky sap from a gum tree. Then he went and hid it deep in the forest, in the place he knew Mmoatia loved to be. And then he chose a hiding place beneath a canopy of leaves and he watched... and he waited...

There was a rustling of leaves, but nothing to be seen. The rustling grew louder and came closer. Anansi felt a brush of wind against his cheek. And then he heard a voice... the voice of Mmoatia.

"Why won't you talk to me?" the voice hissed.

Anansi whipped around. Was Mmoatia talking to him? Then the voice came again.

"How dare you be so rude?"

With relief, Anansi realized his trick was working. Mmoatia was talking to the wooden doll.

"I said SPEAK TO ME!" shrieked Mmoatia, and at that moment, Anansi saw the doll's head move. Something, or rather someone, had touched it. And whoever had touched it, was clearly stuck to it.

"What's going on?" said Mmoatia.

Now the whole doll was moving. It looked like Mmoatia had both hands stuck to it.

Anansi leaped from his hiding place and strung his spider silk around Mmoatia and the doll as hard and fast as he could, until he had wrapped her into a cocoon.

"Let me go! Let me go!" cried the furious Mmoatia.

"Never!" cried Anansi. "For now I will have paid my price." He tucked Mmoatia under one of his arms and slid, whooping with joy, up to the Sky God, on his skein of silk.

"So you have done it," said Nyame. "And the Sky God is not one to break his word."

He handed over the box of stories and Anansi took it with him, all the way back to Earth.

He looked at it for a moment. It was nothing but a carved wooden box, no different from any other box. What would lie inside? He flipped open the lid with one of his legs and out spilled the stories.

Word upon word, filling the air with their hum, they spun out and beyond to the ears of men, and Anansi knew nothing would ever be the same again. He had given stories to the world.

Finn MacCool was a famous Irish giant. Legend has it that he built the Giant's Causeway across the Irish Sea to get to his enemies, the Scottish giants. This is the story of how the Causeway came to be.

Finn MacCool

Long, long ago, when giants roamed Ireland, trampling trees like twigs and tossing mountains about like rocks, there lived one of the greatest giants of them all – Finn MacCool. He was so big and so brawny he thought he must be the strongest giant in all the world, and so he called out with his roaring voice, all the way across the sea to Scotland…

"Benandonner! I challenge you to a fight. I hear you are the fiercest of the giants in Scotland. Well, come and see what Finn MacCool is made of!"

"Challenge accepted!" Benandonner bellowed back. "But how am I going to get over the sea to fight you? I don't want to wet my feet in this freezing sea!"

"Not a problem," said Finn. "A giant of my great size and strength can easily build a bridge across the sea!"

And so Finn set to work. He loped across Ireland, grabbing hulking great rocks in his huge hands and throwing

them out into the water. Then he packed them tightly together, one against the other, making a causeway all the way from Ireland to Scotland.

"Ha!" laughed Finn, when at last he had finished. He looked on proudly at the stones that snaked their way across the sea, topping the waves that crashed and foamed and swelled against their sides.

"That'll show Benandonner," thought Finn. "Not many giants could build a bridge to span the sea. Benandonner will be quaking in his boots when he sees this."

At last, exhausted from his hard work, he lay down on the ground to rest.

As Finn slept, he dreamed... of victory against Benandonner, of being the greatest giant that ever lived. He would become a legend... he would be famous... a hero...

BOOM! BOOM! BOOM!

Finn woke with a start. What was that? Was it thunder? An earthquake?

BOOM! BOOM! BOOM!

The sound was getting louder. And closer. Finn rose to his feet. The ground was shaking and rocks were falling and something was blocking out the sun. Finn looked out to sea and gasped. There, coming across the causeway, was a giant of a giant!

"He's at least twice as tall as me," thought Finn, "and with legs as thick as ten tree trunks and knuckles as sharp as flint and he's carrying a spear as tall as a tower."

And then it dawned on him. This must be Benandonner,

the giant who was coming to fight him...

Finn turned tail and FLED, without stopping, all the way back to Fort-of-Allen in County Kildare.

"I'll never win!" he realized as he ran. "Benandonner will pummel me into a pulp, squish me like a fly. I'll be battered and broken and beaten... What am I going to do? I can't fight him!"

As soon as he reached home, he burst through his front door and called for his wife.

"Oona, Oona," he shouted. "Benandonner, the Scottish giant, is coming to fight me and he's the size of a mountain. What shall I do?"

Finn's wife Oona had a mind as sharp as a spear. She paced the room, cooking up a plan as easily as she baked her bread.

"You must hide in here," she said at last, "and put on these."

"In here? And wear these clothes?" baulked Finn. "Are you sure?"

"Just do as I say," said Oona. And she winked at him and closed the door.

Not long after, the stamping feet of Benandonner could be heard at Kilcock and then at Robertstown, and all the while Oona waited patiently with a secret smile on her face, while Finn stuffed his ears with clods of moss to keep out the sound. Then, at last, came a banging that shook the whole house and Oona opened the door in welcome.

"Where's Finn MacCool?" demanded Benandonner. "I've to come to fight him."

If Finn had feared him from across the sea, then

close-up Benandonner was ten times as terrifying, but Oona never so much as trembled. She looked up into his granite eyes, and his crooked teeth as long as knives, and smiled.

"Oh, it's such a shame," she said, lying without any trace of deceit, "but he's gone over to County Kerry today to hunt some deer. Would you like to come in and wait?"

"I'll wait," agreed the huge giant. "I'm not one to avoid a fight."

"But first," said Oona, "would you like to put your spear down next to Finn's? His is just over there," she added, pointing to a huge fir tree that had been felled by a storm.

With a grunt, Benandonner propped his spear next to the tree and followed Oona through to the kitchen.

"Over there is Finn's shield," said Oona, pointing to a vast piece of oak. "And that's his knife," she added, as they passed the wicked blade of a sword.

"Now, you must be famished," Oona went on. "Let me cook you a meal. I'll make the one Finn loves best."

And she went into the kitchen and pounded the dough, mixing it with iron filings and flints she had hidden in her pocket. And while she baked it into bread, Benandonner waited hungrily, all the while pondering the size of Finn's spear and his shield and his knife.

"What kind of giant is this Finn MacCool?" he wondered. "If his weapons are anything to go by, he must be at least twice my size."

But he said nothing and the thought of food kept him where he was. At last the bread was done and Benandonner bit into it. No sooner had he done so than his two front teeth cracked on the iron filings.

"Oh dear," cried Oona, "I'm so sorry. That's never happened to Finn. Maybe it's because your teeth are so small compared to his."

Benandonner smiled a grim gap-toothed smile and took another bite. This time his back teeth cracked on the flint and he put down the bread with a THUMP!

"Have some meat," said Oona, and she passed him a strap of old leather painted red.

Benandonner chewed and chewed and chewed some more, but there was no way of swallowing it down.

"Never mind about the food," said Oona, taking it away. "It's clearly too much for you. Here, have some honey-beer to drink. You must be thirsty having walked all the way from Scotland."

And she produced a vat of honey-beer big enough to drown a horse.

"Finn would drink this much?" asked Benandonner, eyeing the sloshing liquid.

"Oh no!" laughed Oona. "He'd have double that for breakfast. I gave you less as you're not quite up to his size."

"Hmm," grunted Benandonner. "If Finn can drink this much mead," he decided, "then so can I." And he downed it as fast as he could, until his head grew dizzy and his legs felt wobbly and weak beneath him.

"Now come and see our baby," said Oona.

Bleary-eyed and woozy-headed, Benandonner followed Oona into the next room, where an enormous baby with a bonnet on its head smiled out from a cradle.

Benandonner gasped. That was a baby?

It was over half the size of Benandonner himself.

"Would you like to hold him?" asked Oona, as she cooed and clucked over the cradle.

"I'm not so good with babies," said Benandonner, backing away. "I think, perhaps, yes, I think some fresh air would be good."

Suppressing a giggle, Oona showed him out to the garden. It was peppered with boulders that had rolled down off the mountains years ago, but Benandonner wasn't to know that...

"If you're bored you could play with those rocks," said Oona, pointing at the boulders. "Finn and his friends like to play catch with them. Sometimes he throws them over that mountain and then runs around to catch them before they hit the ground."

Benandonner eyed the boulders warily. "Perhaps I could do it…" he thought.

He placed his huge hands under a boulder and heaved as hard as he could. He just managed to lift the massive stone above his head, but then down it came, back to the ground with a thud.

That was when Benandonner knew. There was no way he was going to beat the great Finn MacCool in a fight. That giant must be the greatest on Earth… the stuff of legends… a hero.

"Thank you, Oona, for all your kindness," he said. "But I can't wait any longer for your husband. I'll have to be getting home now. Of course, I'll be back to fight him another day."

"Of course," said Oona. "I understand. He'll be so sorry to have missed you."

As soon as Benandonner was out the door, Finn leaped

out of his cradle and threw off his bonnet and followed Benandonner to make sure he really had left Ireland. Then he set to work, tearing up the causeway from his end, just as Benandonner made sure to do the same, so that no giant could ever make his way between the two countries again.

This myth explains the origin of the Sun
and Moon. Nobody knows quite how old
the story is, but it was probably first told
in Korea thousands of years ago.

The Sun and the Moon

There was once a time when the sky was dull and empty. There was no Sun to shine in the day nor Moon to glow at night – only a few stray clouds to fill the space between Earth and the heavens, high above.

In that time, there lived an old cook, whose rice cakes were known far and wide as the tastiest in the land. She would wake early each day and spend the morning grinding rice into flour, mixing it with water and kneading it into a soft dough. Then she would steam it, filling the air with the fragrant smell of cooking rice.

"It smells delicious," said Haesik, the cook's daughter. "Can I have some?"

"Only if I can have some, too!" called Dalsun, the cook's son.

Their mother laughed. "Wait until I've finished, then you may both have one." It was the same story every morning, but it always brought a smile to the old woman's face.

After the dough had cooled, the cook kneaded and pounded it, stopping when the dough was springy and her wrists began to ache. Finally, she tore it into little pieces and shaped each piece into a beautiful rice cake.

Before the cook had even finished shaping her first cake,

it was greedily snatched up by Dalsun, who ate the entire thing in one enormous bite.

"Hey!" cried Haesik. "That one was mine." But a second later, her mother handed her a cake of her own. When Haesik bit into it, she sighed with pleasure. "It's so good. Can I have another?"

The old woman shook her head. "I need to take the rest of the cakes to sell at the market," she said, loading the cakes into a basket. "If there are any left at the end of the day, you can both have another."

Haesik and Dalsun glanced at each other and smiled. They knew there would be a cake left for each of them. There always was. So they helped their mother fill the basket with the freshly made rice cakes, then lifted it up so she could carry it easily above her head.

When their mother was ready, she set off for the market.

She staggered up and down steep hills, trudged along muddy roads and cautiously tip-toed across rickety bridges, until at last she saw the market in the distance.

"Not far now," she said, wiping the sweat from her brow. She raised one foot, about to continue, when—

"What is that most delightful smell?" came a gentle purr from behind her.

The cook's spirit soared. "What luck," she thought to herself. "I haven't even arrived at the market, and already someone's interested in my cakes." She beamed a huge smile, turned around, and let out a gasp.

Instead of finding a customer standing there with coins ready to spend, the cook found something quite different. Something twice as large as a normal man. Something with glossy orange and black fur, sharp white teeth, and huge, yellow eyes – *hungry* eyes.

"A t... tiger!" stammered the cook.

"Not just any tiger," the tiger smiled, obviously pleased to have such an attentive and fearful audience. "I'm *the* tiger. The strongest, fastest, most brilliant tiger in all the land.

And if you so much as think about
running away, I'll swallow you
whole before you manage to
take your first step."

The cook's eyes darted
left, then right, then back
again, struggling to think
of a way to escape.

Meanwhile, the tiger
began to stalk a wide circle
around her, sniffing the air as
he went. "What is that heavenly
smell? What tasty treats do you have
for such a great tiger?"

"These?" said the cook, slowly lowering the basket to the
ground. "These are rice cakes. I'm on my way to the market,
to sell them." Then the cook had an idea. "If you let me go
on my way, I'll happily give you one."

"Just the one?" said the tiger, with a mocking laugh.

"One now..." said the cook, lifting one of the cakes from her basket, "...and one every day you let me pass through here unharmed."

The tiger paused his prowling and considered the cook's offer. The longer he thought about it, the more enticing the smell of the rice cakes became. Soon his mouth was watering so badly he felt he had to answer quickly or risk drowning. "Deal," he spluttered. "Now give me my treat."

With the deal made, the cook placed the rice cake in front of the tiger. He eyed it suspiciously, poked it with one claw, licked it once, licked it twice – then took the whole thing into his mouth and chewed it, delightedly. He was enjoying it so much, he hardly noticed as the cook picked up her basket and crept away.

When the cook returned home later that day, Haesik and Dalsun were eagerly awaiting her. "Did you sell them all?" asked Dalsun, taking the basket from his mother.

"I sold all but two," said the cook with an exaggerated sigh. "What should I do with them?"

"I'll have one!" cried Haesik and Dalsun in unison. With a nod from their mother, they reached inside the basket and snatched out the last rice cakes of the day. They vanished almost as quickly as they had emerged, leaving not so much as a crumb.

When the children had finished eating, the cook sent them off to bed. She still had to soak the rice, so it would be nice and soft the next day, ready to be ground, kneaded and steamed. Yet all she could think about was her encounter with the tiger. "I hope I don't see him again," she whispered to herself.

The night passed quickly, moving from an empty, black sky to an equally empty blue one. At once, the cook set to work, preparing the rice cakes for the day. As usual, she gave one to each of her children before heading out.

This time, the cook decided to travel a different path to

reach the market. The journey was longer, and had many more hills to struggle up and down, but extra hills were far better than the risk of being eaten by a tiger. After another hour of walking, she soon spotted the market in the distance. "Aha!" she said.

"Aha!" purred a rather satisfied voice, sending chills running down the cook's spine. She turned around. Once again, there was the tiger.

"I hope you're not forgetting our bargain," said the great cat, licking his lips.

"Of course not!" said the cook, forcing a smile. Just as before, she lowered the basket to the ground, took out a rice cake, and placed it in front of the tiger. "I hope the greatest tiger in the land enjoys his rice cake,"

she said, with a bow. She was about to turn away when the tiger cleared his throat.

"*Ahem*," said the tiger, ever so gently. "I think you've forgotten something."

"I have?" replied the cook, scratching her head. "What could that be?"

"Why, my second rice cake, of course," said the tiger with a smirk.

"Your *second* rice cake?" The cook frowned. "But we agreed on one a day."

"That was to journey along your original path unharmed," the tiger replied, casually. "This is a new path. So this is a new deal."

The cook started to shake her head, but stopped when the tiger let out a low, rumbling growl. Reluctantly she gave him another rice cake, then sped off to the market before he could change his mind.

The next day, the cook returned to her original path,

 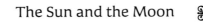

thinking that paying one rice cake was always going to be better than paying two. This time the tiger was eagerly awaiting her.

"Great tiger, please accept this rice cake, as promised," said the cook, placing a rice cake at his feet.

"And the other two?" said the tiger, his eyes fixed, unblinking, on the cook.

"*Two* more?" asked the cook. "But I thought the price for this path was only one rice cake."

"Ah, but it's a new day," said the tiger. "And a new day means a new deal. Today, the price for safe passage is three rice cakes."

This time the cook didn't even try to argue. She placed two more rice cakes on the floor in front of the tiger and walked away. Three rice cakes were nothing when her life was at stake.

But each day, the tiger demanded more and more rice cakes, and each day the cook had no choice but to give in to his demands. It was not long before she was struggling to keep any at all. Yet whenever she returned at the end of the day, she would always manage to save at least two: one for Dalsun, and one for Haesik.

Then came the day when the tiger went too far.

"I want them all," he declared, before the cook had even reached his side. "I am the greatest tiger in the land, and the greatest tiger deserves the greatest treats."

By now, the cook had had enough. "There is nothing great about you," she said. "You are nothing but a greedy, selfish tiger. You take and you take without thinking about how it affects anyone else. Most days I leave here with barely enough rice cakes left to sell. Now, if I give you everything, I'll have nothing left to feed my children at the end of the day."

"Children?" said the tiger, his eyes growing wide. "You never mentioned you had children. The taste of children is so much sweeter than even your delicious rice cakes..."

"Leave them alone!" she shouted, realizing she had made a terrible mistake. But before she could say another word, the tiger opened his mouth wide and swallowed the cook whole, leaving nothing behind but a scattering of clothes and the basket of rice cakes.

"Well, that was a rather bitter meal," said the tiger, wrinkling his nose in disgust. Then his eyes grew wide again, gleaming with mischief. "At least now I know where to find some sweet dessert." With a wicked smile plastered to his face, the tiger collected the discarded clothes and the basket of rice cakes and stalked off in search of the cook's house – and the children waiting inside.

"It's starting to get dark," said Haesik, anxiously, from inside the house. "Mother should be back by now. She always gets back before nightfall."

Dalsun agreed. Something wasn't right. Their mother always returned at the same time each day. "We should lock the door," he decided. "Just to be safe."

It was another few hours before the tiger arrived outside the cook's house. Her tracks had been easy enough to follow. But along the way, he had been so distracted by his hunger, and visions of plump little children dancing in front of his eyes, that he had needed to stop and eat some rice cakes before continuing.

"I need to be careful," he thought. "I don't know how many children are in there. I wouldn't want them to flee before I had a chance to catch and eat them all." He paused for a moment, then remembered the clothes he had collected along with the rice basket.

"Such a clever tiger," he said, praising himself while he put on the cook's outfit. "If I look like that old cook, her children will come to me with open arms."

When he felt his disguise was convincing enough, he walked up to the front door and tried the handle. He shook it and rattled it, but the door would not budge. So he cleared his throat, and in his highest voice, called out: "Children,

I've returned! Be good and let your poor old mother in."

On hearing the voice, Haesik rushed to the window and peered outside. "It's her!" she said, glimpsing the disguised tiger. "It's mother – she's come home at last." She marched over to the door, ready to unlock it, when Dalsun placed his hand on her shoulder, stopping her in her tracks.

"Wait—" he whispered, "—I don't think that's our mother out there."

"It *looks* like mother..." replied Haesik.

"Yes, but listen to her voice. Don't you think she sounds too gruff to be our mother?"

The tiger was starting to grow impatient. "Please hurry along and let me in, children. It's been a long day and I'm ever so tired."

This time, Haesik heard what Dalsun was talking about. Her mother's voice did sound a little rougher than she remembered. But then, the cook did say she was tired...

"Prove that you're our mother," demanded Dalsun, holding Haesik away from the door. "Prove that you're not just some monster, trying to steal us away."

The tiger suppressed a growl. This was proving to be more of a challenge than he had thought. He searched for the basket, then took a cake from inside and rubbed it across his paws until they were covered in white rice dust. Finally, he called out: "Oh, my brave boy. Why would I lie to you? Please, let me in so I can warm my cold and aching hands."

The next thing Dalsun and Haesik saw was what appeared to be a set of white fingers poking through the gaps in the door.

"See, I told you it's no monster!" said Haesik, pulling away from her brother and running to unlock the door. She swung the door wide open, calling out, "Welcome home,

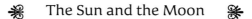

mother... Oh!" For she was face to face with the tiger.

Dalsun pulled his sister out of the way, just as the tiger's jaws clamped shut on the space where she had been standing. The two of them ran as fast as they could, out of the door and into the surrounding woods, the tiger's jaws snapping at their heels.

"Quick, up there!" said Dalsun, pointing at a lone tree in the middle of a clearing. The branches were just low enough for the two of them to jump up and catch them, before scrambling all the way to the top.

"You think climbing a tree will save you?" the tiger boomed. "All you've done is trap yourselves. Now neither of you has anywhere to run, while I have all the time in the world to come up and get you. You might as well come back down so we can finish this sooner rather than later."

When the children refused to budge, the tiger let out a massive sigh. "So be it," he said.

Just as the tiger was hiking up his skirt, ready to climb,

he caught sight of a woodcutter's hatchet leaning against an old log nearby. He gave a wicked grin. "Why should a tiger as powerful as I have to clamber up a tree, when I can make those children come to me instead?" He dropped his skirt and walked slowly and calmly over to the hatchet.

Up above, the children watched the tiger slink away, unsure of what to do next.

Dalsun looked all around him, trying his best to come up with an escape plan. "It's no use," he muttered after a while. "We really are trapped. All we can do is pray to the gods and hope they rescue us. If they decide we're pure of heart, they will send a rope for us to climb up to the heavens. But if they think we're rotten, then the rope they send will be old and frail, and that will be the end of us."

Haesik was terrified by the idea of tumbling to the ground from so high up, but what other choice did she have? She clapped her hands together and began to pray.

A moment later, the tiger came back, dragging the

hatchet behind him. "This is your last chance," he yelled. "Come down, or I'll make you come down."

The children ignored him and continued to pray. So the tiger lifted the hatchet high over his head and brought it down on the tree trunk with a *thunk*, chipping away a chunk of bark. The next swing was faster, cutting deeply into the tree. Soon the tiger was hacking away at the tree with a savage fury, sending chips of wood flying everywhere.

"Brother!" said Haesik, struggling to hold on, as the tree shuddered and shook beneath them.

Now it was Dalsun's turn to be scared, but he tried to hide it. "Don't worry," he reassured her. "I'll protect you. I'll always protect you."

As soon as he had spoken, a rope spiralled down from the sky. It hung there, inviting the terrified brother and sister to climb it.

"Sister, the gods have answered our prayers!" Dalsun cried. "Now, quickly, reach out and start climbing – I don't

know how long the tree will stay standing!"

Without another word, Haesik grabbed hold of the rope and began pulling herself up, into the sky. A moment later, Dalsun joined her.

Down below, the tiger was furious – his treats were getting away. "Well then, if prayers worked for them, then they should work for me, too," he decided. He clapped his paws together and prayed to the gods. Just as before, a rope spiralled down from the sky.

"Aha!" he shouted up to them. "I'll get you yet." And he began scaling the rope, climbing higher and higher, until he was almost alongside the brother and sister.

Just as he was about to reach out one clawed paw to swipe at them, the rope he was climbing broke to shreds and gave way. Just like the tiger, it was rotten to the core.

With a terrible yell, the tiger fell to the ground where he landed with a *thud* and a groan.

But the groan didn't come from the tiger. The moment

he hit the ground, his mouth opened wide and out flew the cook, gasping for breath and covered in rice dust.

"I hope that never happens again," she moaned.

The children continued to climb, until at last they reached the heavens. There, Haesik became the Sun, and filled the day with blazing light, while Dalsun became the Moon, and glowed all through the night.

Finally, the sky wasn't so empty any more. Every day and every night, Haesik and Dalsun would look down at their mother and smile. And every morning and every evening, their mother would leave out a rice cake for them, just as she always had and always would.

In myths from ancient Egypt, the sun
was thought to be the eye of the god, Ra.
It was a powerful weapon, but it was
also a living, thinking being.

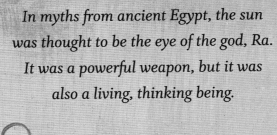

The Missing Goddess

Ra, great god of the sun, was fuming. "How dare she?" he raged, pacing back and forth. "How dare she run off like that? I should never have allowed it – never, never, never!"

"What happened?" asked Thoth, the ibis-headed god of knowledge. He had been summoned to speak with the sun god and had arrived to find him ranting and raving.

"Isn't it obvious?" exclaimed Ra, turning to face Thoth. "My eye has gone! She left me. She transformed into a goddess, as she often does, but this time she's run away to Nubia, where no doubt she's causing a great deal of trouble."

Thoth gasped. Now that the sun god was facing him, it was hard *not* to notice Ra's missing eye. "Um, why did she go?" Thoth asked, trying his best not to stare.

"We argued," said Ra. "I got angry, and then she ran away. Now my powers are weaker than they should be, and if my enemies were to find out – well, I'd hate to think what would happen! Which brings me to why I summoned you here—"

Thoth held back a sigh. He knew exactly what Ra was about to say. He was the god of knowledge, after all. "You want me to go to Nubia, find your eye, in the form of a goddess, and bring her back to you," he interrupted.

"If you would be so kind," Ra replied, with a nod and a smile. "Now go, find my eye, before anyone discovers my weakness!"

In a swirl of feathers and a flutter of wings, Thoth transformed into a magnificent ibis, with feathers as black as night and as white as the Moon. He glided down towards the Earth, swooping across Memphis, the capital of Egypt, over the winding River Nile and far south, to Nubia. Along the way, he kept a careful watch for signs of the missing goddess. What he saw made him shudder.

"So much destruction..." he muttered, passing over towns and villages set ablaze, their statues toppled and buildings in ruins. "The Eye of Ra is truly both angry and powerful. I had better be careful."

When Thoth arrived in Nubia, he remained in the air, soaring over sandy dunes and valleys, on the lookout for the goddess. Finally, he noticed a tiny cat, strutting along in the distance. "Aha," he said to himself, instantly suspicious. "It's not often you see a house cat roaming so far from home."

Instead of flying closer, the cunning god flew behind an outcrop of rock. "Now," he muttered to himself. "How should I appear before her? If I look like a god, she'll know I've been sent by Ra and might attack me on sight. And I can't look like a mere human – not after seeing what she did to those villages."

The god thought long and hard. Then – "I've got it!" he cried, snapping his fingers. In an instant, his arms and legs became short and stumpy, a stubby nose appeared on his face and a tail burst from behind him. In fewer than a dozen heartbeats, he had become a baboon.

With his head and tail held high, Thoth strode over to the Eye of Ra. As he drew closer, he called out in greeting.

"A talking baboon?" purred the cat as Thoth approached. "Such a curious creature." She walked around him, assessing

him without blinking. "You are no ordinary beast. What kind of a creature are you?"

"I could ask you the same question," replied Thoth.

The cat smiled, flashing her sharp, white teeth. "You could, but I wouldn't recommend it."

"What are you doing all the way out here?" Thoth continued. "Surely you'd much rather be at home than wandering this empty place?"

"Home?" the cat replied, suspiciously. Her eyes slowly narrowed. "Ra sent you here, didn't he, to bring me back? Well, I'm not going, and you can't make me."

"Me? You're right. I'm just a baboon. I can't make you do anything," Thoth said. He sat down and scratched himself behind an ear. "But I thought a goddess would behave better."

"What's that supposed to mean?" replied the cat, extending her claws.

"You're a goddess," said Thoth. "You have duties you need to attend to. Without you to help him, how will Ra stop Egypt from falling into darkness and chaos?"

The cat stopped prowling and stood where she was. "He won't," she said rather smugly. "And it serves him right."

Thoth shook his head. Things were not exactly going well. It was time to try a different approach. "Have you thought about how grateful the people will be if you return? There'll be singing and dancing in temples throughout Egypt, with everyone praising your name. You could have any food or drink you wanted—"

"I said no," replied the cat, tartly. "I will not go home. They can suffer in darkness for all I care. Now, really, you're starting to bore me. And I don't like to be bored..."

She licked her lips and suddenly she seemed much larger than she had been before – as big as a man. In fact, bigger – not a house cat at all, but a giant lioness, with fiery tendrils flickering out from her mouth and nose. She let out a great and terrible laugh, louder and wilder than a roaring fire.

Thoth shuddered all over, but somehow managed to keep his voice free from fear when he said: "What a shame it would be for me to die here. Who would be left to tell all the best stories?"

"Stories?" asked the lioness, surprised. She backed away from Thoth and regarded him with newfound interest. "What kind of stories?"

The god smiled, hiding his relief as he quickly thought up a tale. "How about this one," he said, leaping into a story that he hoped would please the goddess, and perhaps calm her down. "Once, many moons ago, there lived a king who had lost all pleasure in life. He longed for a son but he and his wife were childless, so he—"

"Heard it," the cat interrupted.

"How about this one?" Thoth told the lioness story after story. But even if she hadn't heard it already, she simply rolled her eyes through each tale, clearly unimpressed.

As the last tale came to an end, the goddess yawned, revealing rows of teeth, as large and sharp as swords. Thoth was starting to panic. The goddess was unpredictable and dangerous. He could easily imagine those teeth clamping down on his furry little body.

It was at that moment that an idea came to him.

"There was once a mighty lion..." he began, and was relieved to see a spark of interest in the goddess's eyes. "The lion was so powerful that everywhere he went, animals bowed to him in fear.

One day, in the wilderness where the lion lived, he came across a panther who was in a terrible state. His fur was a mess, his tail was bent, and he had scratches and cuts all over his body.

'Who did this to you?' asked the lion.

'Man,' muttered the panther, before slinking away.

'Man...?' the lion wondered aloud. He had never heard of *Man* before. 'I will have to find this *Man* and teach him a lesson,' he decided.

Shortly after that, the lion came across an ox, tied up in a field, with a donkey chained to an old wagon nearby. To each animal he asked: 'Who did this to you?' and both animals replied, 'Man'.

The lion was growing furious. He was the greatest creature in the kingdom. Who did this *Man* think he was, challenging his power?

Suddenly, a mouse darted out in front of him. Faster than the mouse could blink, the lion whipped out a paw and pinned the mouse to the floor. Just as he was about to toss the little thing into his mouth, the mouse let out a loud and terrified squeak.

'No!' she wailed. 'You don't want to eat me. I'm nothing but fur and bones. You've coughed up hairballs bigger than me. Please, let me go, and I promise I'll come to your rescue when you need me the most.'

The lion laughed. '*You*? Rescue *me*?' The idea amused

him so much that he decided to let the mouse go. 'I haven't laughed that hard in a long time,' he said. 'Now run along, little mouse, before I change my mind.'

The mouse scampered away and the lion continued on his quest to punish Man. But the journey was a long and tiring one, and soon the lion grew thirsty. When at last he spotted a waterhole in the distance, he raced over to it, salivating at the thought of cool, fresh water.

But, before he could reach the waterhole, the ground seemed to leap up and trip him, and the lion found himself falling through the air. He was caught in a huge net. Desperately, he tried to get free, but the net closed ever more tightly around him. 'What is this?' he roared.

'Man did it,' came a little squeak of a voice.

The lion tried to look around to see who was talking, but he was too entangled to move. 'Who's there?'

'I am!' said the little mouse. She had crawled up onto the lion's snout, and was fixing him with her little black eyes.

'Man left a trap for you, and you blundered into it. But don't worry, I'll soon have you free.'

The mouse set to work, gnawing and nibbling the strings that held the lion tightly – and painfully – in place. It took a lot longer than the mouse had promised but, eventually, the lion was free.

'Thank you,' said the lion, feeling more than a little embarrassed to have been rescued by such a tiny creature. 'But why are you helping me?'

'Because I promised I'd come to you in your time of need,' said the little mouse. 'And because doing a good deed for someone is a beautiful thing.'

The lion nodded at the mouse's wisdom. He bent down so that the mouse could climb up into his mane, and then together they made their way back to the wilderness, far from the world of Man—" Thoth paused for a moment, then added: "—because the world of Man is a dangerous place, and even the most powerful of creatures can fall prey to

Man's trickery."

The goddess looked at him, no longer through the flaming eyes of a lion goddess, but through the wide, curious eyes of a house cat. "Are you trying to scare me? Or threaten me?" she asked, intrigued. "Am I supposed to be the lion in your story?"

"Perhaps," said Thoth. "Or maybe you're the mouse and Ra is the lion? And without you by his side, there is nobody to protect him from the evils of the world."

The cat hissed. "I am no mouse, baboon." She fell silent, and for a time, Thoth wondered if she really might eat him. Finally, she said: "I will come with you. I have always admired beauty. And if doing a good deed for someone else is beautiful, then I suppose that is what I should do."

Thoth let out a massive sigh. He stood up, trembling only slightly as he did so, and together, the baboon and the cat returned to Egypt.

Just as Thoth had foretold, when they arrived in Egypt,

a huge troupe of dancers and musicians were awaiting them. They struck up a song and soon everyone was singing and dancing, celebrating the return of the Eye of Ra.

The goddess was overjoyed. She quickly shed her cat form and changed into a beautiful woman. She joined the merriment, completely forgetting why she had been so angry in the first place.

When the party ended, Thoth and the goddess were exhausted. They curled up on the ground and at once fell into a deep sleep.

Not long into their slumber, Thoth heard a strange noise, like the raspy whisperings of an old man. Then came an unmistakable hissing. He bolted upright, listening intently while he looked around and sniffed the air with his keen baboon senses. At last he saw it – a huge serpent, dark as night and large enough to swallow the goddess whole, snaking towards her.

"Goddess, wake up! An enemy approaches!" boomed Thoth, his voice echoing through the night.

When the goddess failed to stir, Thoth began to panic. The serpent drew closer and closer, its jaw open wide, its needle-like fangs dripping with venom.

Just as the serpent was about to strike, the goddess rolled over and reached out – not with the graceful hand of a beautiful woman, but with a huge paw, its claws like flaming knives. She struck the serpent a terrible blow, shattering its fangs and flinging it across the land.

When the serpent hit the ground at last, it turned to dust and blew away on the breeze, as if it had never existed.

Thoth looked up at the goddess – once more a lioness – her fur rippling in the air like flames, and smoke billowing from her nostrils.

"You were right," she growled. "Ra's enemies sent that serpent to kill me in my sleep. We should get back to him as quickly as possible. Without me, he doesn't stand a chance."

The goddess took on her cat form once more, and she and Thoth quickly made their way to Memphis. They passed by towns and villages, ignoring every party and festival, until at last they arrived in the capital city and soared up to Ra, waiting in his temple.

"You've returned!" he said, beaming at the sight of them. He turned to the cat and frowned. "I'm sorry that we argued. I hope you will forgive me."

In a burst of fur and whiskers, the cat transformed into a goddess, with two pointed cow horns rising from out of her head. She looked at Ra, then back to Thoth, who had now resumed his own godly form, and she let out a little sigh.

"I forgive you," she said. "And I am sorry, too. I now know what it is like to be attacked when you are vulnerable. I shall never run away from you again and will always protect you. For nobody should be scared to go to sleep at night. Not the largest lion, nor the littlest mouse."

Each year, on the seventh day of the
seventh month, the Chinese celebrate
the Festival of the Double Seventh – and
the reunion of two lovers separated by a
river of stars. This is their story.

The Cowherd and the Princess

Long ago, in China, there lived a poor cowherd named Niu. He had no family and no money, except the few coins he earned looking after other people's animals. One day, as he was walking across the fields, he spotted an ox that had fallen into a deep, mud-filled ditch. It was old and bedraggled, and hardly had the strength to struggle.

"Poor thing," thought Niu. He slithered down into the ditch and pushed and pulled until at last, with a final effort, the ox scrambled free. Cold, wet mud caked its coat, so Niu took a handful of straw and began to rub it down – revealing gleaming, golden hairs. Niu rubbed and scrubbed. When he had finished, the ox shone like gold.

Niu could see this was no ordinary creature. So he was not as startled as he might have been when it spoke.

"Thank you," said the ox. "You are a good man." Its

gentle eyes took in Niu's ragged clothes. "Now it is my turn to help you," it said. "What do you wish for most in the world?"

"A wife," sighed Niu. "But who would want to marry me? I'm just a poor cowherd, and besides,

I never meet anyone..."

The ox smiled. "Hide by the lake tonight and you may meet a princess," it said. "The seven heavenly princesses like to come down to Earth to bathe. They are wary of mortals – but if you steal one of their cloaks, then that princess will stay and talk to you."

Niu thanked the ox, and went to the lake. Patiently he watched and waited. The sun set and the moon rose over the crystal water. He was just starting to wonder if he had dreamed the whole thing when the moonlight grew very bright. Niu blinked... and then there were seven young women in shimmering silk cloaks, each in a different shade of the rainbow. They were the seven daughters of the Empress of Heaven. They were all very beautiful, but the last was so lovely that she made Niu catch his breath.

Her name was Zhinu and her cloak was the soft red of a summer sunset. Her six sisters wore rich golden headdresses, but her long ebony hair was crowned only by a single red peony. As he watched, she dropped her cloak and stooped to dip her slender fingers in the water.

Niu felt suddenly shy. "Still I *must* speak to her," he told himself. He stepped out and boldly seized the red cloak. Six princesses gasped, clutched their cloaks and vanished. The seventh stayed and turned to face the cowherd.

"Please, return my cloak," she said coolly.

"Beautiful princess, Daughter of Heaven, I cannot refuse you," he said. "But may I ask you one question first?"

"What is it?" asked the princess, intrigued.

"Will you marry me?" said Niu, blushing.

The princess laughed at his boldness but she held his gaze, for she had always wondered what it would be like to live on Earth. And besides, there was something about this young man that made her want to try... perhaps it was gentleness, or his look of adoration, but with a nod of her head, she agreed.

So Niu and the princess were married and lived happily

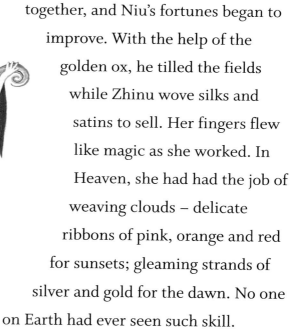

together, and Niu's fortunes began to improve. With the help of the golden ox, he tilled the fields while Zhinu wove silks and satins to sell. Her fingers flew like magic as she worked. In Heaven, she had had the job of weaving clouds – delicate ribbons of pink, orange and red for sunsets; gleaming strands of silver and gold for the dawn. No one on Earth had ever seen such skill.

Before long, they had saved enough to buy their own farm. A little while later, to add to their joy, they had two beautiful children, a boy and a girl, with dark eyes and dimpled smiles.

Time passed, and their only sadness was losing the ox. Just before it died, it spoke to Niu one last time.

"After I die," the ox told him, "you must cut off my hide and keep it. You must then make it into a cloak."

Niu shook his head. "I couldn't do that," he said.

But the ox insisted. "You will need it one day. If you wrap yourself in it, you will be able to fly."

Each year on Earth is but a day in Heaven, so for a while, no one in Heaven noticed Zhinu was missing. But slowly, without her weaving, the sunsets turned dull and drab, and the dawn lost its silvery glow.

"This won't do," said the Empress of Heaven crossly. "Zhinu is neglecting her duty. Where is she?"

She looked around. The princess was nowhere in Heaven... Finally, she looked down and saw her daughter, a heavenly princess – living with a cowherd!

"She has broken the laws of Heaven," raged the Empress. "How dare she! No heavenly being may marry a mortal – and a cowherd? She must come home at once!" And she sent the heavenly guards to fetch her daughter back.

When the guards arrived, Niu was out in the fields and Zhinu was at home with the children.

"You must return to Heaven," they told her. "The Empress commands you! You are needed to weave the clouds."

Zhinu bowed her head sadly. She could not disobey.

"I love you," she whispered, kissing her sleeping children. Then she put on her red silk cloak and vanished.

When Niu returned and found his wife gone, he was devastated. He could guess where she was, and knew she would not have left him and the children willingly.

"I will find her and bring her back," he decided. He tucked their children into a basket, wrapped the golden ox hide around his shoulders and flew up to Heaven after her.

The Empress was furious when she saw them. "No mortal may enter Heaven!" she cried. She took a silver hairpin from her hair and scored a deep line across the inky skies. The line became a river of sparkling stars, deep and wide and impossible to cross.

Zhinu was trapped on one side of the starry river, weaving her clouds, and Niu and the children on the other.

Yet still Niu did not give up. He stayed by the river, weeping for his beloved. And on the far shore, Zhinu wept for him as she wove. The strength of their love impressed everyone in Heaven, even the Empress – and she relented a little. She could not let Zhinu go back to Earth, but she allowed Niu and the children to remain in the skies as celestial beings.

Zhinu still weaves the clouds but, once a year, on the seventh night of the seventh moon, she stops. On that night, magpies fly up and form a fluttering bridge of wings over the starry river – and Niu and the children rush across it into Zhinu's waiting arms. They can spend only one precious day together before they must part again, but the joy of that reunion fills their hearts for the rest of the year.

Hindu mythology is full of sacred
stories and poems about heroic deeds.
This story tells of the creation of the
goddess Durga, born to defeat evil.

The Demon Who Fought a ❧ Goddess ❧

Mahisha was a demon. His father was lord of the underworld, his mother a buffalo woman, and he was born half-man, half-buffalo. He could switch between the two in the blink of an eye and take on the form of any animal he chose.

But Mahisha was also proud and vain. He lived for power and pleasure and was always greedy for more. To get it, he prayed and fasted for many months until Lord Brahma, creator of all things, appeared before him.

"I want to live forever," Mahisha demanded.

"You were born mortal and must remain mortal. All who are born must die," Lord Brahma replied.

"Then let it be only at the hands of a woman," said Mahisha. "No god nor animal will be able to kill me." And Lord Brahma promised him it would be so.

Believing he was invincible, Mahisha raced to the underworld and called to the demons gathered there. "The gods are powerless against me," he declared. "Let's rise up against the people on Earth."

The demons cheered. As a vast, red-eyed army they marched to Earth, where they slaughtered their way from one kingdom to the next. Soon, Mahisha was king of all the Earth. He ruled with terror, and the people quaked with fear.

But no sooner had Mahisha conquered the Earth, than
he set his sights on the heavens.

Indra, king of the gods and lord of the heavens, saw him
coming. "Do we fight or run?" he asked the other
gods. They chose to stand firm and fight. Indra
mounted his seven-trunked elephant. Lord
Brahma called for his flying
swan, Lord Vishnu his
flying eagle and Shiva
his magnificent bull.

As Mahisha and his army
converged on the heavens, Indra raised
his thunderbolt and smashed Mahisha's
mace, and the battle began. But just as the
gods thought they were winning, Mahisha encircled them,
and began attacking from all sides. His army turned into
buffaloes. They kicked with their hooves and gouged with
their horns. The gods were forced to retreat. They fled to the

mountains and forests and Mahisha took the throne. "From now on, everyone must worship me, and me alone."

In secret, the gods gathered together at Lord Shiva's home. "What shall we do?" asked Indra. "How can goodness overcome evil?"

"Only a woman can stop him," confessed Brahma, remembering his promise. "But it is not our custom for women to fight. How will Mahisha ever be defeated?"

"It is time to invoke the Mother of the Universe," said Lord Shiva. "Only she can stop Mahisha."

The three great gods opened their mouths until light streamed out, and in the light a woman appeared. She was formed of the gods' anger and their power, but she was stronger than any of them. She shone with the brilliance of a thousand suns. She was beautiful and ferocious and her name was Durga. She had hundreds of arms, and into her outstretched hands, the gods gave their weapons – a trident, a thunderbolt, a sword, a conch, a mace, a discus, a baton, a beating stick, a cleaver, a javelin, a snake, a bow... The god of the winds gave her a quiverful of the sharpest, swiftest arrows. Yama, god of death, gave her a noose and the god of the mountains gave her a lion to ride on. Then Durga roared until the Earth shook and the seas swelled.

"Please," begged the gods, "we have created you to destroy evil in the form of the demon Mahisha."

"Have no fear," Durga replied. "I will annihilate him."

Then she rode to the top of a mountain... and waited.

Mahisha had heard the roars that shook the Earth and for a moment, he was afraid. "But a mere woman cannot defeat me," he told himself. He ordered his army of demons into battle. Knowing she could not face them alone, Durga created an army from her own breath. Each fighter was as brave and ferocious and patient as Durga herself.

The battle seemed never-ending. Mahisha realized he had to face Durga alone. So he transformed into a buffalo and charged, head lowered, horns gleaming.

Durga's lion reared up, tearing and scratching, while Durga threw her noose around Mahisha's neck. As she raised her sword, Mahisha changed into an elephant. With his long, strong trunk, he pulled at the legs of the lion, trying to throw Durga from her mount. But Durga held aloft her sword, ready to bring it down on the elephant's trunk.

Mahisha changed into a lion and then into a buffalo again, only for Durga to make a deep wound in his side. Mahisha knew that to survive he would have to change his form, and fast. But just as Mahisha was half-emerging from his buffalo form, Durga's lion leaped on his back and pinned him down. In one final movement, Durga brought down her sword, and Mahisha was no more.

The gods were overjoyed. They fell at Durga's feet. They praised and blessed her. They celebrated with flutes and with drums, with sitars and bells.

"Go now, in peace," said Durga, "for goodness has triumphed over evil."

The first horses appeared in North America
over 250 years ago. Historians say the
horses came from Europe, but a tale from
the Blackfoot tribe tells a different story...

The Water Spirit's Gift

Long ago, there were no horses in North America. The people there had never even seen a horse. Tribal chiefs didn't ride proudly across the prairie and hunters didn't gallop through the countryside, chasing juicy buffalo to eat. When people moved from camp to camp, they struggled with their heavy packs and their bodies never seemed to stop aching.

At that time, there lived a boy named Achak. He had a big heart and an even bigger yearning for a better life. All he could remember were long, harsh winters which seemed as if they would never end. Even the coming of spring didn't help much. The buffalo were still hard to find.

One night, the elders of the tribe sat around the campfire, worrying.

"Another day, another disappointment," muttered one. "How are we supposed to catch buffalo when they can run twice as fast as us?"

"I don't know how we'll survive if the spirits send us another bad winter," grumbled another.

Everyone in the tribe believed in spirits. Spirits decided between feast or famine, good health or terrible disease.

Just beyond the light of the fire hid Achak, listening to every word. His big heart ached for his tribe. He tried to trust the spirits, but things were so tough, he couldn't help but wonder if the spirits had abandoned them.

It was too much to bear. "Something must be done," he said to himself. "And I shall be the one to do it."

Achak crept to his tepee and gathered up a spare pair of moccasins and his raccoon-fur cap. Then he slipped away across the prairie, as silently as if he were stalking a rabbit, until the red glow of the campfire was lost in the darkness behind him.

Achak kept walking through the night and on into the next day. He walked to the edge of the prairie and beyond, through hills rustling with sweet grasses. He listened hard in case the spirits were trying to talk to him. They would give him a sign soon, he knew it.

It was getting dark again when Achak stumbled down the side of a hill and saw something shimmering in front of him. He rubbed his eyes. It was the Great Lake. The water stretched as far as he could see. It could have been the end of the Earth for all Achak had a chance of crossing it. He had walked so far, and now he could go no further.

In despair, Achak slumped to the ground. His shoulders shook as his tears flowed.

All around the lake, animals stopped what they were doing and pricked up their ears to hear the strange sound. They had heard their own babies mewling or squawking or squealing, but they'd never seen or heard a boy before. Together they went to investigate: the mother wolf crept, the eagle swooped, the bear ambled and the otter poked her head above the water to see what was going on.

The animals weren't the only ones who heard Achak sobbing. In the middle of the Great Lake lived Water Spirit, who was old and very powerful indeed.

"What is that noise?" Water Spirit asked his son, Tashunka. "Go and find out for me."

Tashunka sped away towards the shore, his feet gliding across the water like a canoe.

"What's the matter?" he asked kindly, when he found Achak sitting in despair on the bank.

Achak didn't raise his head. "I've been wa-walking all day and night," he sobbed. "I wanted to do something to help my tribe, and I've fa-failed."

Tashunka put a cool hand on Achak's back. "Don't cry," he said. "My father can help you. He lives in the middle of the lake."

Now Achak glanced up – and gasped. The boy standing above him looked like no one he'd ever seen before. The boy's hair was as slick as otter's fur and his body glistened as if covered in shining scales.

"My father is Water Spirit," Tashunka continued. "He owns all the animals that live in the lake and around it. He might offer to give you one to help your tribe."

Achak's mind worked fast: which animal should he ask for? The eagle could fly ahead of the hunt and let the hunters know where buffalo were grazing. Or the wolf? She could run for miles and catch rabbits for them to eat.

But Tashunka hadn't finished. "If my father offers," he said seriously, "you must ask for the oldest duck in the lake."

Achak was confused. Why would he ask for an old duck, when there were so many other animals? But if this boy really was a spirit's son, Achak knew he should trust him.

"How am I going to get to the middle of the lake?" he asked Tashunka, standing up. "I can't swim."

The shining boy smiled. "Hold onto my shoulders and close your eyes."

Achak held onto the boy's shoulders, his eyes tight shut. Again, Tashunka ran across the surface of the lake. Achak whizzed behind him, his toes barely touching the water. In the middle of the lake, Tashunka held tightly to Achak's hand and plunged into the water.

As they dived down together through the glistening water, Achak discovered with astonishment that he could breathe under water. He held tightly to Tashunka, hoping that the magic would last long enough for him to meet Water Spirit.

Tashunka led him to a huge tepee, green as seaweed and strung all over with shining pearls. Inside sat Water Spirit. Achak noticed the shimmer of his skin and the bow and arrow slung over his shoulder, made from delicate fish bone.

"Why are you here?" Water Spirit asked, his loud voice echoing around the bed of the lake.

"I want to help my tribe," Achak said bravely. "However hard we work, our lives never get any better."

Water Spirit blew bubbles thoughtfully.

Then, just as his son had predicted, he made Achak an offer: "I'll give you any one of the animals who live in or around the lake – just take your pick."

Achak remembered Tashunka's advice. "I'd like the oldest duck you have," he said.

Water Spirit chuckled. "Are you sure?" he said. "Why not the otter? He could catch enough fish to feed you all like kings every day. That old duck isn't worth a thing."

The otter did sound good… but Achak shook his head. "The oldest duck, please," he repeated firmly.

"As you wish," replied the spirit. "You're wise beyond your years. My son will take you back to the edge of the lake and give you that old duck. But when you leave to return

home, you mustn't look back until daylight."

Achak and Tashunka sped back to the shore. There, on her nest, was the old duck. Half of her feathers had fallen out and the rest were scruffy and tattered. Achak started to wonder if he'd made the right choice... But it was too late now. Tashunka braided together marsh reeds to make a rope and tied it around the duck's neck.

"Remember," he warned, as he handed Achak the rope. "Don't look back until daylight."

Achak set off towards the camp, the old duck waddling behind him. His head was spinning with everything that had just happened.

It was still dark when he reached the prairie again. Then, he felt a sudden tug on the rope. He had to grip hard to stop it from slipping through his fingers – and as he gripped, he saw the rope change in his hands. What had once been marsh reeds transformed into thick leather.

Achak stared at the rope in his hand in shock. He ached to look back to see what was going on, but he resisted. Water Spirit's warning had to be obeyed.

He even managed to stop himself from turning back when the soft padding of the duck's feet and the swish-swish of her feathers changed into something completely different, like an elk's hooves on the baked earth.

And that wasn't all: the old duck was making strange snorting noises. The noises got louder and louder, until thudding hooves and loud snorting filled the entire prairie.

In the east, the sun peeked over the horizon. But still Achak didn't look back. He didn't want to risk breaking the Water Spirit's spell.

The camp was just visible in the distance when the sun broke free of the land. It was definitely daylight now.

Finally, Achak turned around...

There, in the sunlight, stood a magnificent creature. She had four legs like an elk, dark eyes like an otter and a smooth coat like a hare, but she was taller than a man. Her back looked strong as a buffalo's, and her legs were long and agile. She pawed the ground with shining hooves and shook out her long mane.

Achak gazed at her in complete wonder. Her dark brown eyes met his and she took a shy step forward. Achak took a step forward too, his legs shaking right down to his moccasins. Slowly they approached each other, until they were close enough for her to nuzzle his neck with her soft, velvety nose.

So entranced had Achak been with the gentle creature in front of him, that he only then looked around for the first time. An entire herd of the amazing creatures was standing on the prairie. Although Achak didn't know it yet, these were the first horses in North America.

Gently, Achak began to lead his horse towards the camp. With a toss of her head, she gestured for the others to follow behind.

"Look, it's Achak!" someone yelled from the camp. "But what in the name of the spirits are those?"

Very gradually, the members of the tribe came onto the prairie. They stared in wonder at Achak and his horses.

They had never seen anything like it.

"Water Spirit has helped us. Our problems are over!" said Achak, proudly. "Look how strong they are! And I bet they're quick too. You could catch a buffalo easily riding one of these."

Everyone's eyes shone with delight as they got to know their new companions. The horses seemed so calm and friendly. One man approached the horse nearest to him and lifted his little daughter up onto its broad back, where she sat waving and laughing with joy.

From then on, the tribe and their horses lived happily side by side. They learned how to braid the horses' manes and tails with bright yarn and feathers. During the day, the hunters sped bareback across the prairie and at night, the camp feasted on buffalo while the horses grazed peacefully around them.

On those nights, Achak sat by the fire, singing and laughing with the rest of the tribe. One day, he would become chief and his adventure with Tashunka and Water Spirit would be just one of many. But that was in the future. For now, his big heart was happy and he was at peace.

In Japan, stories of mischievous spirits
abound. This myth, set over 800 years
ago, tells of a *kitsune* – a fox spirit
that gets up to no good.

The Fox Maiden

Genno was a wise Buddhist priest. He was also a restless wanderer. Through summer sun and winter snow he made his way across Japan, never settling in one place for too long.

One hot summer's day, Genno was striding across the great Nasuno Plain, already sweltering under the heat of the afternoon sun, when the wind abruptly dropped. Until now, the cool breeze had made the heat bearable, but without it, the poor priest was starting to suffer.

"I need to get out of the sun," croaked Genno, his throat dry. He looked around for some shade, but the nearest trees were small dots in the distance. He was about to give up hope when he noticed a huge stone, jutting up behind a stretch of susuki grass. Wearily he lumbered over to the stone and collapsed in its shadow.

"Beware!"

The voice came as if from nowhere. Genno, thinking the heat had addled his brain, looked around in panic.

"The stone before you is no ordinary lump of rock. It is the Death Stone. All who touch it, whether human, beast or bird, will die," the voice proclaimed.

"From a mere touch?" gasped Genno, realizing it was the stone itself that was talking to him. "And who are you, to tell me such things?"

"I am a spirit, as restless and as trapped as you are. But while you suffer under the scorching sun, which will soon disappear below the horizon, I must remain here for the actions of my past, which can never be undone."

Listening to the spirit of the Death Stone sparked Genno's curiosity, and he begged the spirit to tell him its story from the very beginning.

"As with all such stories, it begins long ago," said the spirit, "when a woman of unmatched beauty and grace arrived in the court of the Emperor. Light shimmered across her fine black hair, her robes shone bright with all the hues of the land, and she smelled as sweet as cherry blossom.

Her name was Tamamo-no-Mae, and her beauty was only matched by her intelligence. Everyone at court found her fascinating, but nobody more so than the Emperor himself.

Often the Emperor would call her to his side, testing her with questions on Buddhist lore, science and ancient poetry. Her every answer was wise and full of understanding, spurring even more questions from the intrigued Emperor: 'At night, when the skies are clear and the stars emerge, we may see what they call the *Milky Way*. But what is it really?'

'That is for gods, not men, to know,' said Tamamo-no-Mae with a smile. 'But were I to guess, I would say it is the spirit of the clouds, spread above us.'

The Emperor was struck by her honesty and the beauty of her words," the spirit went on. "He continued to seek out her company, becoming more and more entranced by her wit and charm.

One evening he invited her to a performance of music in his private chambers. His heart leaped as she arrived, gliding into the room with the elegance of a heron in flight.

Together they sat behind a set of bamboo blinds, in some privacy from the ministers on the other side, to talk and relax between each score of music.

But as the final performance was drawing to an end, an odd thing happened. From absolute stillness came a sudden blast of wind, strong enough to blow out the fires of all the lanterns, plunging the room into darkness. Then, just as suddenly as the wind, there came a faint glow. The Emperor turned towards it and saw Tamamo-no-Mae, shining as though she were daylight itself.

The light spilled through the bamboo screen and filled the room, much to the shock and awe of the ministers on the other side. But rather than feeling fear, the Emperor thought Tamamo-no-Mae radiated with beauty.

'Incredible!' he gasped. 'Surely you are no ordinary human, but some divine being.' From that moment on, he promised to keep her by his side forever more–"

"But where do you fit into all of this?" the priest interrupted. He had been listening to the spirit's story with great interest, but now his curiosity was beginning to outstrip his patience. "And how did your actions lead to you being bound to this stone?"

"The answers to those questions are to be found in what happened next," replied the spirit, its voice as light and airy as the summer breeze that had returned, whispering through the tall grass.

"Not long after the night the lanterns had failed, the Emperor fell gravely ill. The doctors were baffled as the Emperor's strength waned with each passing day. Soon he was barely able to lift his head from exhaustion. The chief physician prodded and probed him, fed him various remedies and covered him in ointments. At last, he decided that the Emperor had been contaminated by evil, and that no man-made cure would work.

At once, the palace fell into a fury of prayer. Every man, woman and child prayed to spirits and gods alike for the Emperor's life. But nothing changed. Fearing the worst, the Emperor sent for his beloved Tamamo-no-Mae.

When she arrived at his chambers, she fell down beside him in distress. His skin was tight and slick with sweat, his eyes were cloudy and pale, and his every breath seemed a struggle.

'Tamamo-no-Mae,' the Emperor wheezed, 'it is a pity that I will have to leave you soon. I had thought our journey was just beginning, but now it seems it's at an end...'

'No!' cried Tamamo-no-Mae. 'I will never leave your side. Not until I breathe my last breath.' Then she turned to the head physician and asked, 'There must be something that you can do?'

The head physician thought long and hard. Finally, with little to lose, he sent for a fortune-teller, to see whether *his* skills could shed some light on a solution.

The fortune-teller's name was Abe-no-Yasunari, and upon his arrival he was quickly ushered into the Emperor's chambers, where Tamamo-no-Mae was waiting. There, he told the Emperor's fortune, and at once let out a gasp.

The doctors surrounded him, eager to learn what secret he'd discovered, but Abe-no-Yasunari refused to say a word. It was only when the court ministers came along and took him to a private chamber that he revealed the truth of the Emperor's mysterious illness.

'It is the woman, Tamamo-no-Mae,' whispered Abe-no-Yasunari. 'She is not what she seems. Her very presence in this palace is a blight upon the Emperor's health. Remove her, and all will be as it once was.'

'But, what is she?' asked a wizened minister, stunned by

the fortune-teller's announcement.

'She is under the influence of an ancient evil,' the fortune-teller continued. 'It is hundreds of years old and full of malice. It aims to shorten the Emperor's life so that it may take over as ruler.'

The ministers' gasps at this revelation soon turned into outbursts of rage at having been deceived by such a being. They rushed to the Emperor's side, urging him to do something about Tamamo-no-Mae. But the Emperor refused to believe them. How could so heavenly a woman be evil? He was about to dismiss them when Abe-no-Yasunari – who had arrived late, having tottered along behind the outraged ministers – spoke up.

'Your majesty, you are clearly no fool – though affection for your beloved Tamamo-no-Mae seems to have blinded you. Have you not noticed that she is gone? And I'll tell you why. It's because the woman you claim to be so heavenly knew what I would see when I cast your fortune. She knows too what will happen to her if she stays, and so she has fled, back to the Nasuno Plain, where she came from.'

Upon hearing the fortune-teller's words, the Emperor used what little strength he had to sit up and search around the room. There he saw ministers, doctors, the fortune-teller – but Tamamo-no-Mae, the woman who had promised to remain by his side, was nowhere to be seen.

He fell back to his mattress with a deflated thud and gazed up at the ceiling, holding back tears. At that moment, the Emperor's heart hardened, and with a whisper he demanded: 'Summon the greatest warriors of Japan. Have them hunt down Tamamo-no-Mae, that I may regain my health and never be tricked by such a being again.'

The ministers wasted no time carrying out the Emperor's order. They beseeched the legendary warriors Kazusa-nosuke and Miura-nosuke to bring an end to Tamamo-no-Mae, ordering them to leave immediately, in case the woman returned to finish what she had started.

'For the Emperor!' cried the warriors as their hunting party charged from the palace, their horses snorting fiercely as they went. Out across the Nasuno Plain they rode, searching frantically for Tamamo-no-Mae.

Now and again the warriors would glimpse bright silk robes billowing in the distance, or the sheen of dark hair amidst the tall grass. They would spur their horses into a gallop, calling out wildly to one another not to let Tamamo-no-Mae slip away. But whenever they closed in on her, she did just that, disappearing completely before anyone could get a clear look at her.

After days of this, the warriors were exhausted. Refusing

to go home, they set up camp on the edge of the plain and took turns sleeping.

'I can barely keep my eyes open,' said Miura-nosuke when it was his turn to rest. He could feel his eyelids drawing closed. 'I could sleep for...'

'...Hours? Years?' asked a woman's voice, as soft and wild as sea foam.

Miura-nosuke's eyes burst open, and there, in the middle of the camp was Tamamo-no-Mae, glowing like the sun, with golden tears streaking down her pale face. He went for his sword, but try as he might, he could not move.

'Is this a dream?' he gasped.

Tamamo-no-Mae smiled, though her eyes remained sad and full of tears. 'Tomorrow, by your hand, I will be no more. Please,' she begged, 'spare me my fate.'

But despite her tears, Miura-nosuke would not bend. He had given his word, and he would not break it. Instead, he went again for his sword. This time his hand obeyed him, darting to the hilt of his blade. It was at that moment the dream ended, and Miura-nosuke's eyes erupted open to the sight of Kazusa-nosuke looking wearily down at him.

'You have slept for too long,' said Kazusa-nosuke. 'We must continue our hunt, or else we will return to our families in shame.'

Together, the warriors set off once more across the Nasuno Plain. They had not gone far when Kazusa-nosuke let out a mighty cry: 'There!' he boomed, pointing out the rainbow robes of Tamamo-no-Mae.

Within the space of a heartbeat, Miura-nosuke drew his bow, plucked an arrow from his quiver and took aim.

Sensing the warriors had her in their sights, Tamamo-no-Mae ran across the land, picking up speed as she went.

Faster and faster she sped, until the force of the wind tugged the robes from her body, revealing not a woman, but a giant fox, larger than any horse, its nine tails rising and

falling behind it like silk on a breeze. It was ready to leap over a great stone, to disappear in its shadow, when Miura-nosuke released his finger on the bow string.

The arrow flew far and true. It struck the fox mid-leap, sending it tumbling down to the stone..."

"This very stone," concluded Genno, knowingly. "And here you've dwelt ever since."

A long silence stretched out before the spirit replied. "You have guessed correctly, wise priest. I am the spirit that took the form of Tamamo-no-Mae, and this stone has been my prison since the moment the arrow struck. Here I must remain, alone with my sadness and the memories of my wrongdoings."

Genno could hear the misery and regret in the poor spirit's voice and knew it was no trick. While some may say the priest was a fool for what he did next, the truth is he was a good man and hated to see another being in such pain.

The priest went to his belongings and, from inside a

small bag, he removed a stash of incense. He burned it in front of the stone and recited sacred scriptures with his hands pressed tightly together. Finally, he intoned: "Spirit of the Death Stone, I ask that you be released from your bonds, that you may tread the world once more, in search of peace and forgiveness."

It was growing dark now and all was silent when, with an almighty crack, the Death Stone split in half. There was a flash of light, brighter than even the midday sun, forcing Genno to turn away. When he looked back at the remains of the Death Stone, he found himself looking up at an enormous fox, staring at him with unblinking eyes.

"You have freed me, kind priest," said the fox spirit. "Now I may run and dance once more. For that, I must thank you." And with a powerful kick of its hind legs it leaped away, soon vanishing into thin air.

Genno rose to his feet, gathered up his belongings and returned to his wandering ways. He never found out what became of the fox spirit after that day, or whether or not it returned to its mischievous habits. Perhaps in the end it was happy enough with its freedom, and to this day is leaping and darting across the plains of Japan in peace.

For the indigenous peoples of Alaska, myths often explore the relationships between people, the natural world, and a powerful, overlapping spirit world.

The Origin of the Winds

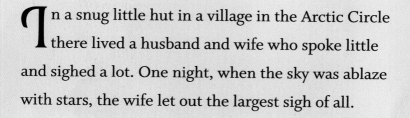

In a snug little hut in a village in the Arctic Circle there lived a husband and wife who spoke little and sighed a lot. One night, when the sky was ablaze with stars, the wife let out the largest sigh of all.

"How wonderful it would be to have a child of our own, to love and spoil during these long, silent nights," she said, pausing only once to clear her throat, for it had been a long while since she had last spoken.

If the husband was startled by his wife's sudden words, he did not show it. When he replied, his voice was tinged with sadness. "It would be a wonderful thing to have a child, who we could tell stories to and laugh with when the light of day has passed. But we are simply too old. We will never have a child of our own."

There the conversation ended, and nothing more was said until, days later, the wife once more cleared her throat and asked: "Husband, will you make a boy for me?"

This time the husband's brow furrowed and his eyes grew wide in shock. "You want me to do *what*?"

"Beyond our village, deep in the frozen tundra, I have heard of a single tree that glistens with light. Will you visit the tree, remove a piece of its trunk and from it, carve us a boy that we can love as our own?"

The husband thought long and hard about his wife's request. He thought for so long that soon the day passed to night, and only then did he reach a decision.

Without a word, he pulled on his thick fur parka and sealskin boots and set out into the dark. He strode beyond the village borders and deep into the tundra, just as his wife had instructed. There he came across something he had never seen before.

Stretching out in front of him was a broad ribbon of light as bright as the moon, forming a long, winding path across the snow-covered ground.

The husband was seized by curiosity. He followed the path for what seemed like forever, accompanied only by the sound of snow crunching underfoot. Hours went by until at last he arrived at a solitary tree, glimmering like sunlight reflected on water.

"This must be the one," said the husband, gazing at the

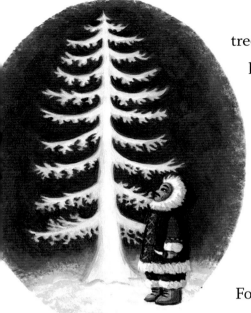

tree in awe. He took out his hunting
knife and carefully cut out a piece
from its trunk. Then he made his
way home, back along the path
of light.

When the husband
returned with the piece of wood
in hand, his wife was delighted
– but his task was far from over.
For what was left of the night, and
long into the following day, the husband
whittled away, shaping the wood into the doll
that would be their son. He ate no food and drank little
water, intent on finishing what he had started.

"He's beautiful," whispered the wife hours later, when
the doll was complete and her husband was slumped in his
seat, his discarded tools by his side.

Carefully she took the doll into her arms and cradled it,

remarking over its little arms and legs and its round, smiling face. "Finally, we have a family," she beamed. With a nod, her husband smiled wearily back.

Next, the wife made the doll some tiny fur clothes and had her husband carve a little knife and dish from the leftover scraps of wood. They gently placed the doll on a bench, put food on its dish, then, overcome with tiredness, they went to bed.

Most of the night passed in peaceful sleep until, all of a sudden, the wife woke with a start. "Husband! Husband!" she called, shaking him from his well-earned sleep. "Do you hear what I hear?"

The husband listened. There was a low whistling sound spreading through the hut. "What is that?" he groaned, exhausted from all his efforts the day before.

"It's the doll – I'm sure of it!"

Slowly the couple made their way to the bench where they had left the doll. To their surprise, the wooden dish in front of it was completely empty. More than that, the doll turned its head and looked at them, its eyelids blinking, its little hands waving, and its mouth curled up in the biggest smile they had ever seen.

"Now our family really is complete," said the wife. She picked up the doll and swung him around and around, laughing in joy.

Together the couple and the doll played games, told stories, laughed and sang until they were too tired to keep their eyes open. So, with the doll tucked snugly between them, the couple soon fell fast asleep.

But when they awoke in the morning, the doll was gone.

"Where is he?" cried the wife. "Who has taken our boy?"

The husband searched the hut, calling out for the doll. Then he flung the front door wide open and stepped out into the snow. "Dear wife," he said, sheepishly, "I don't think anyone has taken our boy. Look at these tiny tracks in the snow. He's run away on his own two feet."

The husband and wife hastily donned their thick winter furs and left the warm hut and the little village in search of the doll. They followed his footsteps across the tundra until they arrived at the path of light. There the footsteps vanished. The wife burst into tears.

"Don't worry, dear wife," consoled the husband. "Our son will return to us, I'm sure of it. All we can do is wait and hope he comes back soon." And the couple turned around and slowly wended their way home.

Meanwhile, the little doll was walking merrily along on the path of light. He skipped and he danced, enjoying his life and his freedom. As he went, his eyes darted about excitedly, amazed by this newfound world. He was so distracted by the world around, behind and beneath him that he failed to notice a strange wall rising up directly in front of him.

"Ouch!" the doll cried, skipping blindly into the wall and falling backwards. "What was that?"

Looking up, he realized he had reached the edge of day,

where the sky meets the Earth. And there, attached to the sky wall was a strange patch of hide, bulging as if something strong on the other side was pushing at it, causing it to flap and rattle loudly.

"What a curious thing," said the doll. "It's certainly very quiet out here. I think it would be a good idea to let a little more noise in." So he took out his wooden knife and cut a hole in the patch of hide.

WHOOSH! At once a powerful torrent of air surged through the hole, howling as it came, and causing the doll to cling to the sky wall for fear of being blown over. Then came a reindeer – and another – leaping through the open hole.

"What in the world—!" exclaimed the doll. "What kind of thing are you that pushes and blows with such power?"

The little doll waited for a reply, but all he could hear was howling.

"Maybe if I can see where the air is coming from, I'll be able to work out what it is," decided the doll. So he grabbed

The Origin of the Winds

hold of the patch on either side of the hole, pushed his head through and gasped. On the other side of the sky wall was a second world, much like the Earth.

In that second world, the howling was different. Rather than a meaningless noise, the doll heard a powerful, booming voice calling out, "I am the wind of the east. Hear me roar, hear me howl, louder than man, child or beast...!"

Shocked by what he had heard, the doll pulled his head back into his world and carefully closed the patch of hide. Then he whispered to the wind on the other side. "East wind, you are welcome to visit our world whenever you like – but you are a powerful force. So when you do come, sometimes blow hard, sometimes blow lightly... and sometimes, do not blow at all!"

Excited by his discovery, the little doll continued on his journey along the edge of day until he came across another patch of hide, bulging out from the sky wall. With a flick of his knife, he cut loose the edges and at once a great gale swept in, bringing with it reindeer, trees and bushes.

Just as before, the doll stuck his head through the hole, and there he heard the wind singing, "From the southeast I gale, bluster and gust, bringing pieces of trees and clouds of dust...!"

On hearing this, the little doll tugged the hole closed and whispered, "Southeast wind, great as you are, you are simply too strong. Sometimes blow hard, sometimes blow lightly... and sometimes, do not blow at all."

From there the doll headed south until he came across another hide patch in the sky wall. This time, when he cut a hole in it, he was blasted by a hot wind bringing spray and foam from a huge sea on the other side.

The doll stuck his head through the hole and listened to the wind, while he stared out at the giant arching waves. Then he closed the hole and whispered, "South wind, I welcome you to our world, but sometimes blow hard, sometimes blow lightly... and sometimes, do not blow at all."

The little doll hurried to the west, and then to the northwest, discovering in each place another hide patch. From the first sprang the west wind, bringing rain and sleet and soaking the poor doll's clothes. The wind from the second patch was even fiercer, blasting the doll with ice and hail. In both instances he quickly closed the holes and whispered what all the other winds already knew.

When the little doll started towards the northern part of the sky wall, he found himself slowing down, struggling with the extreme cold. He felt it seeping into him, freezing his joints and chilling him to the core. Soon the cold made it difficult to think, let alone move. So the little doll retreated, to warm himself in the south wind.

Yet he was still determined to head north. So once his joints were thawed and his mind was clear, he buried himself deeper into his furs and set off again. This time, he stayed near the middle of the world until, from a great distance, he could just make out the northern patch of hide.

Then he charged straight towards it, ignoring the cold as it pinched at him.

Finally he reached the sky wall, and there he cut a small hole in the hide patch, releasing the north wind. It howled and it raged, screaming its name amidst a torrent of ice and snow, threatening to blow the tiny doll across the world.

At once, the doll snapped the patch shut, demanding of the wind, "North wind, you are great and powerful, but you are too quick to freeze. You are only to come to this world in the middle of winter, when people will expect you, so they will never be caught off guard by the sharp cold you bring. Even then, sometimes blow hard, sometimes blow lightly... and sometimes, do not blow at all."

With all the winds released, the little doll wandered back to the middle of the world. There he lay down on top of a tall hill and rejoiced at the sounds the winds made through the grasses and trees.

Then the doll gazed up and noticed that he was lying

directly beneath the top of the sky, where he could see dozens of arches joining together, much like the poles of a tent. He lay there, watching the blue fabric of the sky ripple gently in the breeze. For a while, the doll simply rested, enjoying the change that he had brought to the world. But after hours had passed, he knew it was time to go home.

"My parents must be very worried," he said, feeling more than a little guilty at having run away. He stood up, dusted himself off, and started walking.

When the little doll arrived home, the husband and wife threw their arms around him, squeezing him so tightly he thought they were angry with him and trying to crush him. But when they let him go, he could see tears in their eyes and smiles on their faces. "You've returned to us. How we've missed you," they said in chorus before making him tell his story from start to finish.

From that day on, in that snug hut, in that village in the Arctic Circle, the husband, the wife and the doll lived a happy life together. Their evenings were never quiet, but always filled with stories, songs and laughter. And if ever there was a sigh, it was never uttered by the couple. Instead it came from the winds outside, gusting and breezing through their new world.

'The Children of Lir' is a famous Irish legend
which is part of a whole cycle of stories
which tell of the settling of Ireland and
the adventures of the gods.

The Children of Lir

Long ago, the Tuatha De Danaan ruled in Ireland. They were gods and goddesses of the tribe of Dana. They were full of music, laughter and dancing and had learned the secrets of magic.

Among them was the great sea god, Lir. His wife had died, leaving him with four children, Fionnuala, Aodh, Fiacra and Conn, whom he loved very much. But still Lir was lonely, and he came to marry again. His new wife was named Aoife and at first they were happy. Aoife was as beautiful as the mellow season, with her russet red hair and her hazel eyes. But Aoife's love for Lir soon turned to jealousy, to bitter anger and then to hatred. She couldn't bear how he doted on his children, how much they were loved by all the Tuatha De Danaan and by everyone in the kingdom. Her hatred began to possess every part of her until she was forced to take to her bed and stay there.

Lir visited her often, terrified he would lose another wife. But Aoife mistook his attention for pity, and it only enraged her all the more.

For a year, Aoife lay in her darkened room, plotting terrible deeds and hatching plans like a demon in the shadows. At last, she decided what she was going to do.

"This," she thought, "will win me Lir's love again, and this time it will be all for myself."

Aoife waited until Lir went away on a hunting trip, and then she leaped from her bed. She ordered the coachmen to ready the carriage, called for her stepchildren and announced a visit to Killaloe, where their grandfather lived.

All the children ran to the carriage, but Fionnuala, the eldest, hung back. The night before she'd had a dream that her stepmother had placed a terrible curse upon them. But there was no getting away.

Her stepmother hustled her into the carriage, and the horses set off, galloping through the rolling countryside.

They camped that night by the shores of Lake Derravaragh. "This is it," thought Aoife. "This is the place. I'll kill the children and Lir will be mine. All mine."

But when the moment came, and the children of Lir lay sleeping at her feet, she couldn't bring herself to do it. So she waited till morning and invited the children to swim in the lake. They stripped off their clothes and rushed to the water. As each child passed her, Aoife touched them with a magic rod and chanted under her breath:

Three hundred years on this lake
Three hundred more on the Sea of Moyle
Three hundred on the Western Ocean
That knows no bounds but the sky
Until the woman from the south
*   weds a man from the north*
And the cold bell peals on the wind.

As soon as the children touched the water, they turned into wild white swans. And all at once, Aoife regretted what she had done, but she knew the curse could not be undone. So she cast a second spell, giving the swans human intelligence and human speech and the sweetest of voices for song. Then, without thinking, she carried on to Killaloe, where the children's grandfather lived.

"Don't say a word," she hissed to the carriage driver.

When they arrived at the grandfather's, he rushed out to greet them. "Where are the children?" he asked, seeing Aoife alone.

Aoife made up a story about leaving them at home, but the carriage driver had loved the children of Lir and couldn't hold his tongue. "She has turned them into swans," he whispered.

The grandfather turned on Aoife with a howl of rage. He grabbed hold of his magic rod and turned her into a spirit of the air, never to be seen again.

When Lir returned and heard the news he was distraught and wept for three days.

The Tuatha De Danaan gathered together on the shores of Derravaragh, listening by night to the sweetest singing, and talking by day to the children of Lir.

"Come home," begged their father. "Come, Fionnuala; come, Aodh; come, Conn; come, Fiacra." He stroked their soft white feathers. "I cannot give you back your shapes till the curse ends, but come back home, white children of my heart."

Conn looked at him with his huge black eyes and shook his head. "We have the voices of your children," he said, "but the hearts of wild swans. The dusk calls to us. We wish to spend the nights on the water, with the waves lapping at our sides."

Then Lir covered his eyes in sorrow and blessed his children. "May your wings bring you joy from the air and your feet be glad in the water. Farewell, Fionnuala, white

blossom; farewell Aodh, red flame of my heart; farewell, Conn, that brought me gladness; and farewell, Fiacra, my treasure."

The children of Lir rose into the air. They felt the wind in their feathers and they stretched their necks to the freedom of the sky.

The swans lived on the lake and their father often came to see them. The villagers came to hear them sing and in spite of their feathered form, they were happy. Three hundred years passed and then they flew to the Sea of Moyle, driven on by their curse.

But the Sea of Moyle was cold and the children of Lir were hungry. The waves tossed them about and the sea swirled around them. As the clouds gathered low, they could tell a great storm was coming. "Let's choose a meeting place," said Fionnuala, "in case the waters divide us."

So they chose the Rock of the Seals. That night, the storm raged across the waters. The children of Lir were hurled through the air and lashed by the waves and, though they cried out, their voices were lost to each other in the tempest.

By morning, with broken feathers and bruised wings, Fionnuala headed for the Rock of the Seals, and there she sat, alone. Thinking her brothers and sisters had drowned beneath the pounding waves, she sang a sad lament. "Oh, come to me, Conn. Come to me, Aodh. Come to me, Fiacra."

And across the waters came Conn, on sea-soaked wings, and Fionnuala covered him with her wings and they warmed each other.

"If only Aodh and Fiacra would come," she said. "There would be no bitterness in my heart."

And from across the waves came Aodh and Fiacra. And they sheltered on the rock until the sun came and made their feathers bright again.

For three hundred years they lived on the wild and inhospitable Sea of Moyle and then they left for the Western

Ocean, urged on once again by the curse. The storms were even fiercer there than on the Sea of Moyle. But at last three hundred years were over. "We can go home again!" cried the children of Lir. They flew across Ireland and looked down for all the places they had once loved, but they were all lost to them, vanished like the white mists of morning. There was their childhood home, now a crumbling pile of rock, without light or music or warmth.

The swans slept that night in the long grass, silent with grief. When morning came they saw strangers living on the land, where the Tuatha De Danaan had once danced

to music and hunted the silver stag.

"Even the mountains have no life in them," said Conn, as they lay upon them, silent and sorrowful.

"But wait," cried Fionnuala, pressing her ear to the grass. "They may be dark but they are not dead. Listen! I can hear the beating of their mighty hearts. Let us tell them our story, then they will pity us and we will not be alone."

So the children of Lir sang their song to the mountains all day until the skies grew dark. And when they came to the end of their story they lamented, "We have nothing left but you and the earth of Ireland."

Then the swans cried out as they saw mountain after mountain light up from within, and the strains of faerie music hung for a moment in the air.

"The De Danaans are still alive," said Fionnuala, "and our father's house is hidden now where old age cannot wither it."

From across the hills they heard a church bell ringing and they remembered their stepmother's curse. They followed the sound of the bell and found a little hermitage on the shores of Killaloe, where they had spent such happy times as children. And word spread of the beautiful swans with the soaring songs, until it came to the ears of a princess from the south, who was to marry a prince from the north. The princess demanded to own the singing swans and set out to fetch them. But as soon as she reached out to touch them, Aiofe's curse finally came to an end.

Their swan-feathers crumbled to powder, and the bodies of Lir's children became no more than a handful of dust. But as for their spirits, they flew to freedom, to join the Tuatha De Danaan in the Land of the Ever Living.

The story of the children of Lir was not forgotten. It was told again and again by the people of Ireland, and such was their love for the children of Lir that a new law was passed, that no one was ever to hurt a wild swan.

The ancient Babylonians believed in
many gods and goddesses. One of the
most powerful was Ishtar, goddess
of love, new life – and war.

Ishtar & the Land of the Dead

Deep inside the Earth, beneath the oldest cities and greatest seas, there was once a land of dust and shadow called Irkalla, where the living could not enter, and the dead could not leave.

Few people ever journeyed to Irkalla. First, most people had no idea where it was or if it even existed. Secondly, those bold enough to seek it out often spent their lives wandering down endless passageways, risking the perils of falling rocks and gaping chasms concealed by darkness. And if any were unlucky enough to stumble across the entrance to the fabled land of the dead, it never ended well for them.

Irkalla was, for most people, a land they would only ever see after they died. Most people, that is, except for Ishtar. But then, Ishtar was no ordinary woman.

Ishtar was goddess of love. She was more beautiful than anything in the earthly world, and many times more powerful. And she had a wish to visit Irkalla, where her sister was queen. She had never seen her sister's kingdom and despite being the goddess of love, she never felt she had the love of her husband, Tammuz. Maybe, she hoped, he would miss her while she was gone. He might even follow her to the gates of death themselves.

She marched through pitch black tunnels, across deep, cavernous rivers and leaped great canyons on her way to Irkalla. Not once was she tripped by the uneven ground, splashed by the raging waters or so much as scuffed by the jagged walls.

Soon an enormous gateway rose from out of the gloom before her – easily taller than a dozen men and far more ancient than all their years combined.

"Finally," said Ishtar, "the entrance to Irkalla."

She cleared her throat and called out, "Gatekeeper, hear me. I am the great goddess, Ishtar. Open the gates, for I am here to visit your ruler, Ereshkigal – queen of the dead and my own dear sister."

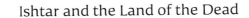

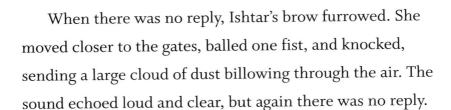

When there was no reply, Ishtar's brow furrowed. She moved closer to the gates, balled one fist, and knocked, sending a large cloud of dust billowing through the air. The sound echoed loud and clear, but again there was no reply.

Ishtar was unimpressed.

"Gatekeeper, hear me," she bellowed. "I am the great goddess, Ishtar. Open the gates, or I shall break them down. I will wrench the lock, smash the planks, put my fists through the posts and tear them to pieces. I will free the dead and let them walk once more in the world above."

As she spoke, her voice grew louder and louder, until her final words erupted from her with such force that the stones in the walls groaned and shook in response.

"No! Please, don't do that!" squeaked a small, muffled voice from behind the gate. "Give me a moment. Let me speak with Queen Ereshkigal and see what she has to say."

Ishtar nodded. Her hair rose and fell around her like crashing waves. Her skin seemed to glow in the dark, and her sharp eyes sparked fiercely like a match about to ignite. If she had to, she would tear down Irkalla's walls with her bare hands.

The gatekeeper sped to the heart of Irkalla, startling Ereshkigal when he burst into her throne room in a fit of gasps and shrieks.

"What is it? What has you in such a state, gatekeeper? Speak!" she ordered.

"Your Majesty... Queen Ereshkigal... goddess of the underworld... ruler of the house of shadows," he panted, "your sister is at the gates. She demands entry into Irkalla!"

"What!" boomed Ereshkigal, leaning forwards in her throne. "Ishtar is here? But why? What is she thinking?" She slumped back, unsure of what to make of her sister's unexpected visit.

"Your Majesty..." said the gatekeeper, after several minutes had passed in silence "...I fear if we delay too long, she will do as she said and tear the walls to the ground."

"The walls?" said Ereshkigal, trying and failing to stay calm. "The walls are the least of our worries! If Ishtar's down here, then who's bringing love to the world above? I don't know what my sister is thinking, coming here, but the sooner she's back where she belongs, the better. Allow her inside – but make sure she pays the price to enter. Everyone must follow the laws of Irkalla."

The gatekeeper hurried back to Ishtar. He found her standing where he had left her, tapping one foot impatiently on the floor, her eyes narrowed to slits. He caught his breath, cleared his throat and announced, "On behalf of our lady of the dead, Ereshkigal, I hereby invite you into our fair land. May it rejoice at your visit."

From out of thin air, the gatekeeper produced a tiny bone key. He slotted it into a hidden lock in the door, twisted it one way, then another, until a tiny *click!* came from somewhere inside.

Ishtar was not a patient goddess. She also had incredibly good hearing. The moment she heard the lock click open, she grabbed both doors and heaved them apart. They groaned in protest, but she simply tugged harder, until she almost tore them from their rusty hinges.

"There we are," she said, when the doors were wide open and she could clearly make out the look of shock on the gatekeeper's face on the other side. She strode through the gate, feeling rather smug. But, as she did so, the strangest thing happened. From out of nowhere, a ghostly hand swooped in and swiped the crown from her head.

"What is the meaning of this?" she cried, turning on the gatekeeper.

"It is the price that must be paid for entering Irkalla," the gatekeeper replied with a smile.

Try as she might, Ishtar could get no further answers

from the gatekeeper, so she carried on through the darkness, muttering as she went. She could not have taken more than a hundred steps before her path was blocked by another gateway, identical to the first.

"How is this possible?" she moaned. "Have I walked in circles? What trickery is this?"

"There is no trickery here," squeaked another gatekeeper, his voice as small and muffled as the first had been. "This is the second of seven gates. Each has been unlocked for you, and you must pass through each, the same as every dead person."

Ishtar frowned. Canyons had shrunk before her, mountains had parted and rivers had waned – how dare anyone or anything block her path? Did they not know who she was?

With a fierce snarl, she took hold of the great doors and savagely wrenched them open, feeling the wood crunch and splinter between her fingers. She passed through the

gateway and, just as before, a ghostly hand appeared, this time plucking out her earrings before fading into nothingness.

Ishtar marched ahead to the next gateway, and the next, losing an accessory here, a piece of clothing there. When she finally passed through the last set of doors, she found herself completely bare. With nothing left to lose, she stormed into Ereshkigal's throne room in a fury.

"What game do you think you're playing?" demanded Ishtar and Ereshkigal at the same time. "What am *I* playing at?" they continued in unison. "What are *you* playing at?"

Ereshkigal held up one hand to quieten her sister. "What were you thinking, coming down here? This is my kingdom. Yours is in the world above. While you're down here, who helps men and women find love? Or helps new crops and animals grow and prosper?"

Ishtar gritted her teeth. "I have never been to your kingdom before, sister. I came here to see it with my own eyes. Is that so wrong? And now you've stripped me of my clothes and my dignity." She glared at Ereshkigal, her eyes wide and full of rage. "If that is how you choose to treat your guests, then clearly you do not deserve to sit on that throne!"

In a flash, Ishtar surged towards her sister, her hands outstretched, ready to drag her to the ground.

But as powerful as Ishtar was, she was far away from her own kingdom. She was in Irkalla now. And while Ereshkigal ruled there, nobody had the power to challenge her.

Before Ishtar could get within an arm's reach of Ereshkigal, swarms of servants appeared, surrounding Ishtar until even the goddess, with all her divine strength, could not move.

Ereshkigal shook her head from side to side. "So be it, sister.

You want to see what my kingdom has to offer? I will grant you your wish. I will see you plagued by every disease in the land until you draw your last breath. And you will remain here forever, as my prisoner."

With a gesture, she ordered her servants to take Ishtar to the dungeons.

Weeks passed, and the world above soon began to suffer from Ishtar's absence. People shied away from each other in the streets, loving couples refused to speak to each other, and no seeds grew in the earth. Eventually the gods learned what had become of Ishtar, and it fell to wise Ea to find the solution.

Ea scraped the dirt from his hands, picked the grit out from under his nails and kneaded it all together. Then he folded it and tweaked it and breathed life into it.

"Your name is Asushunamir," said Ea, "and you are my servant. I have no power in Irkalla, so you must go to Ereshkigal on my behalf. Tell her to end this nonsense.

Ishtar must be set free and the world restored to normal."

Asushunamir nodded, then leaped from Ea's hands and fell to Earth. There, the god's servant quickly set off to Irkalla, never once pausing to rest.

"Open the gates," Asushunamir demanded at the entrance. "I have been sent by the gods above, with a message for Ereshkigal. Only a fool would deny me."

"Not again..." the gatekeeper groaned. He let out a heavy sigh before running off in search of Ereshkigal. When he found her, she was not pleased.

"It seems everyone wants to come to my kingdom these days," she huffed. "Well, let the servant in. The usual way."

The gatekeeper did as he was told, and Asushunamir entered Irkalla, walking through all seven gateways before arriving in Ereshkigal's throne room.

When Ereshkigal set eyes on the servant, she gasped. Never before had she seen such a lovely being. She gazed at Asushunamir's glossy hair, big, bright eyes and youthful skin.

"You're beautiful," she blurted.

Asushunamir smiled, and the world seemed to light up. For a time, the two forgot all about Ishtar. They told stories and played games and laughed at each other's jokes. But Asushunamir could not forget Ea's command forever.

"Your Majesty," said the servant, "I was sent here because the gods above demand that you free Ishtar."

Ereshkigal's eyes narrowed. "I see," she said. "So it was not enough for the gods to make their demands of me, they had to send you, too, to soften my heart. Fine. I will free my sister, but not without a price. She may leave here, but only if she finds someone to take her place. If she fails, she will be dragged back to Irkalla."

With a clap of her hands, Ereshkigal sent her servants to bring Ishtar to the throne room. When her sister appeared in front of her, the queen of the dead took out a bulging waterskin.

"What is that?" asked Ishtar, confused.

"This, sister, is the water of life – the only thing that can bring a person back from death."

Ereshkigal removed the stopper from the waterskin and splashed Ishtar with its contents. Then she told Ishtar about the price she had to pay to stay in the world above and, with a wave of her hand, she ordered her to leave. "Go," she said, "while you still can."

Without so much as a backward glance, Ishtar fled from Irkalla. As she passed through each of its seven gateways, her clothes and accessories came back to her.

Soon she was as beautiful, as powerful – and as clothed – as she had been before she set out on her quest. But her trial was not over yet.

"Who can I choose to take my place?" said Ishtar, knowing what would happen if she failed to find someone to replace her in Irkalla. "Nobody deserves an eternity in Irkalla because of me."

Feeling exhausted and defeated, she returned home,

where she discovered Tammuz, her husband, lazing on her elegant throne.

"Husband, I have returned from the dead. Are you not pleased to see me? Why did you not come for me?"

"You were gone?" said Tammuz, raising one eyebrow.

"Yes, I was gone. For weeks on end. Didn't you notice? Didn't you ask where I was, or even so much as shed a tear for me?"

"I... uh..." said Tammuz, unable to defend himself.

Ishtar felt a great rage rising within her. But rather than shout or strike at her husband, instead she called out to her sister: "Ereshkigal, hear me. I have found my replacement. Take Tammuz, my husband, in my place."

Suddenly Tammuz was surrounded by hordes of Ereshkigal's servants. Before he could utter a word, he was whisked away into the dark halls of Irkalla.

And so it was that the great goddess Ishtar returned to the world above, having confronted the queen of the dead and survived to tell the tale.

*The Aesir and the Vanir were the gods and
goddesses of Norse mythology. This tale tells
of the war between them, and of their
other great enemy... the giants.*

The Wall of Asgard

Asgard, home of the Aesir gods, was once circled by a thick strong wall. But then came the great battle between the two tribes of gods – the Aesir against the Vanir. The sky rained spears, and spells, potent with destruction, were hurled down from the heavens. By the end of the war, the wall lay in ruins. What had once seemed so safe and strong was no more than scattered rubble.

The gods feared that their enemies would soon be upon them, and they had many – the mountain trolls and frost giants; Jormungand, the serpent who circled the world; and the foul creatures who ruled over the realm of the dead.

So when a figure on horseback rode over the rainbow bridge to Asgard and offered to rebuild the wall, it seemed too good to be true.

And it was.

"In return for my help," said the visitor, "I want the sun and moon, and the goddess Freya's hand in marriage."

The gods gasped. This stranger would take light and warmth from their skies so they'd be left to fumble about in

darkness, but worse still, he wanted Freya, their most beautiful goddess, who shone as golden as the sun.

"I'll build the wall higher and stronger than before," swore the stranger. "I'll make you a fortress no giant will ever be able to break down. Just give me eighteen months to complete my task."

"Impossible," barked Odin, ruler of the gods.

"Let us at least discuss it," said Loki, the shape-shifter.

"No!" cried Freya, aghast. "I'll not be bargained for..."

Odin held up his hand to silence her.

"Wait here," he commanded the stranger. And he beckoned the others to follow him to Gladsheim, the vast hall of the gods.

"What did you have in mind, Loki?" he asked, when the mighty oak doors were firmly shut and barred.

"Let's tell him the deal is on if he can do it in six months," Loki replied. "He'll never manage it, and then we've won.

We'll have no price to pay and at least the wall will have been started."

The gods shifted uneasily. No good ever came of listening to the trickster Loki, but it was tempting...

"Agreed?" said Odin, looking around at the other gods. He wanted their approval. Thor, the thunder god, was away in the east battling trolls, and he wanted the Aesir behind him... in case Thor returned and didn't like what had happened.

"Agreed," said the Aesir, and they returned to the waiting stranger.

"You have six months," Odin told him. "Today is the first day of winter. If you can complete the wall by the first day of summer then Freya is yours, along with the sun and the moon. But, if any stone is left unlaid, you come away with nothing. And no one can help you."

"Impossible!" said the stranger. "No one can build the wall in that time.

"Then the deal is off," said Odin, beginning to walk away.

"Wait!" the stranger called after him. "I'll agree, as long as you let me have my stallion, Svadilfari, to help me."

"No," urged Freya. "You cannot risk it. You can't do this to me."

"I don't see how his stallion will help him that much," said Loki. "Go on, agree to his terms, Odin."

For a moment, Odin, the wise one, hesitated. Then he shook hands with the stranger. "The wall is yours to build," he said.

The stranger looked at Freya for a moment, then turned to go. The next morning, the gods watched from the crumbling walls of Asgard as, far below, the stranger toiled like a man possessed. His great rough hands pulled up chunks of rock from the earth. He carried with him a vast mesh net which he tied to his stallion, and hefted the rocks into it, with roars and guttural grunts.

"I can't believe his strength," said Odin. "Of all the gods,

only Thor could move rocks like that."

When the net was full, the stranger slapped his stallion on the back and it began to move, hauling the rocks over grassy mounds and plains and up to Asgard.

"Have you ever seen a horse of such strength?" said Odin. "It's pulling mounds of rocks as if they were pebbles."

And as Freya watched, she wept. "He's coming for me. I know it. This is your doing, Loki."

But Loki just shrugged and said, "It's early days yet."

All through the winter, when the snow fell in drifts and it felt as if the air itself might freeze, the stranger worked night and day to finish his task. By spring, the wall was waist high, and as spring rolled towards summer, it rose higher still, its towering peaks looking like a fortress once more.

"Only the entrance to go," said Freya, "and the wall will be complete. And what will happen then? I'll be his bride and the sun and moon will be gone forever from our skies. You have to stop him."

"This is your doing, Loki," said Odin.

"You signed the deal," muttered Loki. "All I did was suggest it."

But the gods were massing against him. "It will be a horrible death for you, Loki, unless you can stop this stranger."

Loki saw they meant it and his fear made him promise. "I'll stop him," he swore.

The next morning, as the builder drove out with his stallion, Svadilfari, to gather stones, a young mare skipped out of the forest. She pranced up to the stallion, whinnied, and pranced away again. Svadilfari followed. He galloped after the mare,

who slowed for him, then ran ahead. When the builder realized what had happened, Svadilfari was already deep in the forest.

"Come back!" he bellowed. He spent all day and all night chasing his stallion, and got no work done. When morning came, he realised he would never complete his task in time.

He stormed up to Asgard, knowing he'd been tricked, and in his rage he revealed himself to be... a giant.

"We make no deals with giants," said Odin. "You are our sworn enemy. I owe you nothing. Not the sun, not the moon and certainly not Freya."

And Odin called for Thor, the thunder god, to come and help them fight. Thor stormed up the rainbow bridge, swinging his hammer, and repaid the giant with a blow to his head.

As for Loki, he returned some time later, and the gods who watched him closely could have sworn there was something of a horse about him, for the way he occasionally whinnied, and pranced.

Many stories from Polynesia – a group
of islands in the Pacific Ocean –
feature a powerful hero and cunning
trickster known as Maui.

The Fish of Maui

W hen Maui was born, countless lifetimes ago, nobody would have suspected he was destined for greatness. In fact, he was born so frail his own mother, Taranga, thought he was dead.

239

With a heavy heart, she wrapped Maui in a knot of hair cut from her head and left him on the shore for the ocean to claim, weeping fiercely as she walked away.

Maui would certainly have met his end there and then, but the gods of the sky and sea took pity on him. They reached out with arms of wind and surf and, with great care, covered him in a cocoon of seaweed, foam and jellyfish.

"Now at least he will be safe from the crashing waves, biting insects and circling birds," they decided.

True enough, the cocoon kept Maui safe from the dangers of the shore, but it did nothing to satisfy his hunger. Soon his belly was grumbling and growling like a wild animal. He balled his little fists, squeezed his eyes tightly shut, and let out the first cry of his life – and there was nothing frail about it.

"What in the world was that?" said Tamanui-ki-ti-rangi, Maui's grandfather, who by luck, or fate, was passing by the shore. He was a wise and powerful man, and it was not unusual for him to wander the island while he contemplated the great mysteries of life. Yet never before had anyone had the nerve to interrupt his ponderings.

Tamanui-ki-ti-rangi followed the noise to its source and was alarmed to discover Maui, wrapped in frothy foam, soft seaweed and harmless jellyfish. He took Maui into his arms and rocked him gently, but the boy continued to cry.

"There is no need for tears, little Maui," whispered Tamanui-ki-ti-rangi. "You were born so weak, yet alone you have survived the perils of the seashore – and surprised your grandfather by doing so. That is no easy thing to do."

As Tamanui-ki-ti-rangi continued to rock him back and forth, whispering soft words, Maui's tears and sobs began to slow until at last he stopped crying altogether.

Tamanui-ki-ti-rangi smiled. "You will live, little Maui, and you will be a greater man for all your hardships." Then, with Maui in his arms, he made his way home. There he fed him, clothed him, and raised him like his own son.

By the time he was a grown boy, Maui had learned much from Tamanui-ki-ti-rangi, including the ancient secrets of magic. But as much as he loved and respected his grandfather, he was troubled. He could not forget his past, and longed to discover what had become of his mother.

"Grandfather," he said one cloudy day. "You have been so good to me, but now I must return to my mother's house, to reclaim my rightful place as her son."

Tamanui-ki-ti-rangi nodded sadly. "So be it," he said. "You are old enough to decide your own path in life. I will not hold you back, though you will be missed."

After packing up his possessions, Maui waved goodbye to his grandfather and set off home.

Upon arrival at his mother's house, Maui was shocked to discover she was not alone. In fact, she had four other sons – his older brothers: Maui-taha, Maui-roto, Maui-pae and Maui-waho. They watched him warily as he approached, unsure of what to make of him.

"Stay back," warned Maui as they gathered around him, cracking their knuckles and considering him through narrowed eyes. "I have come from the house of your grandfather, Tamanui-ki-ti-rangi, and am no ordinary boy."

One of the brothers threw back his head and let out a long, deep chuckle. "How could such a small boy be anything out of the ordinary?"

But his laugh quickly ended when Maui's hands and fingers stretched and flattened, his face grew small and pointed, and within the space of a heartbeat, what had been a human boy had now become a bright red bird.

The brothers gasped as Maui transformed into one bird after another – one second a white pigeon, the next a tiny robin, or an orange-breasted fantail – until the brothers were so impressed by Maui's powers that they ushered him inside to show him off to their mother.

There, in front of Taranga and all his brothers, Maui revealed who he was and what had become of him from the moment Taranga had left him on the shore.

At first, Taranga shook her head, unable to believe what Maui was saying. But by the end of his story, her eyes were sparkling with tears. She took Maui into her arms after so many years apart, and welcomed him to her home.

Back under his mother's roof, time passed quickly. In fact, it passed too quickly. Maui soon noticed how his family and all who lived nearby, struggled each day to complete, or even begin their chores. By the time everyone had eaten breakfast and set out to work, the sun had already crossed the sky, leaving everyone scrambling about in the dark.

"This won't do," said Maui. "The sun moves too fast across the sky."

Resolved to slow the sun in its journey, Maui visited his grandmother, Muriranga-whenua, whose knowledge of magic was vast and ever-growing.

"You have quite a challenge ahead of you," said Muriranga-whenua, scratching her chin in thought. "But I may have just the thing to help you."

With a flick of her wrist, Muriranga-whenua removed her lower jawbone as easily as if she were plucking a hair from her head.

"Take this," she said. "It is infused with my magic. When you confront the sun, it will not bend, it will not break and even the sun's rays will be unable to resist its strength."

Maui thanked his grandmother. Then, jawbone in hand, he returned home. There he gathered his brothers to his side and told them of his plan. On his orders they wove together several enormous lengths of rope, each longer than a dozen men stacked head to toe. On each end, they fashioned a huge noose, wide enough to circle the broadest of trees.

Together, Maui and his brothers trekked across the land until they reached the edge of a great pit. It was from there that the sun rose each day, to dash and leap across the sky.

The brothers lay in wait, tightly clutching their ropes, until, at last, the sun emerged, erupting from the dark pit in an explosion of light.

"Now!" Maui boomed over the roar of the sun's flames.

At once, the brothers lassoed the sun with rope after rope, encircling its fiery body and gleaming rays, holding it firmly in place.

Then Maui surged forwards, running up and across each rope as if it were a bridge. When he was within arm's reach

of the sun, he raised his magic jawbone and brought it down on one of its many rays, shattering it to pieces. Then he moved on to the next ray, and the next...

"Stop, stop! Please..." cried the sun, struggling to move and feeling its powers fade with every shattered ray. "I will do whatever you wish, just please let me go."

"I will let you go," said Maui, his arms crossed, "if you promise to walk calmly across the sky, instead of rushing, with no mind for the people who toil below."

The sun went mulishly quiet for a moment, and was about to answer back, when Maui lifted his jawbone once again, and...

"Stop! I give in," cried the sun. "I promise I will walk across the sky. Now, will you let me go?"

"You have my word," said Maui, smiling to himself. He retreated back down the ropes, calling out to his brothers that the deal was done and they could let go.

The Fish of Maui

One by one the brothers released their grip, until only one rope remained in place – just long enough for Maui to reach the Earth. When that final rope slipped free, the brothers watched as the sun leaped into the sky. At first, it looked as though it was about to speed off, but then it glided slowly on its way.

From that moment on, Maui was hailed as a hero of his people. He was indeed a great man, as his grandfather had foretold. But over time, the admiration went to his head. He ignored his brothers' requests to help them fish and do the daily chores and instead spent most of his days sleeping.

One day, when his brothers returned from a hard day at sea, Maui went to them, to claim a fish for his dinner.

"You have become lazy, young Maui," said his oldest brother, slapping a fish from his hand. "I will share no food with you until you have proven your worth."

Maui was outraged. Did they not know who he was? He

stormed off and sulked for days, until his belly grumbled and groaned. Only then did he decide that perhaps he should do something about it. Early the next morning he picked up his magic jawbone and hid in the bow of his brothers' ship.

Later, when the brothers pushed their boat out in search of fresh fish, they were completely unaware that Maui was hidden away on board. It was only when they were deep at sea that the young stowaway revealed himself.

The brothers were not impressed. "Rather than come and join us like an equal, you hide and lurk aboard the ship. What a silly thing to do. For that, you can stay where you are. Do not make a sound and do not move until you are ready to be useful."

Maui was really fuming now. Not only had his brothers called him lazy, but they were treating him like a child. So he decided to play a little trick on them. Under his breath he muttered a few ancient words of power, and suddenly the ocean seemed to stretch out longer than before. The brothers paddled and paddled, but they didn't seem to be getting anywhere.

"What trickery is this?" said the eldest brother. "No matter how hard we paddle, we remain in the same place."

Many minutes passed without any progress, until finally the brothers admitted defeat. "Let us turn back. Perhaps we

will have better luck fishing closer to land," they decided.

The brothers turned the ship around and set off. This time Maui said nothing, and the journey was swift and easy.

When they arrived at the fishing ground, everyone took out their fishing lines and bait and began casting for fish. Everyone, that is, except for Maui.

"I suspect you had something to do with our earlier struggles," said Maui's oldest brother. "Because of that, none of us will give you any bait. If you want to catch a fish, you will have to do so with your own two hands."

Maui frowned. He was hungrier than he had been in years, and now he had earned the anger of his brothers, too. But without bait, how could he prove his worth to them?

He looked down at the magic jawbone and suddenly had an idea. He took the jawbone and cut the tip of his nose ever so slightly, so that a drop of blood ran out. "There," he said to himself, smearing the blood across the jawbone. "That will be my bait."

Then he connected the jawbone to the end of a fishing line and tossed it into the ocean, where it quickly sank out of sight. Almost at once, he felt something tug on the line. Something big.

"I've got a bite!" cried Maui, now struggling to hold the line. A moment later, the boat lurched in the water. Maui's brothers shouted for him to let it go – it was *too* big. But instead, Maui began to recite another spell, this one to strengthen the rope and to keep the fish on the line.

Maui pulled and heaved while his brothers looked on,

dumbfounded. Finally, in an explosion of water, a great fish broke the surface. Except this fish was completely flat and covered in emerald green grass. In fact, it wasn't a fish at all. It was land. New land. The brothers were speechless. Maui was not.

"There, brothers. I have brought forth the greatest fish – a new land for us to divide between us. But it is no more ordinary than I am. This land is sacred, and you must not touch it until I return with a priest to bless it for us."

Before the brothers could protest, Maui transformed himself into a bird and with one, two, three flaps of his wings, took to the air, leaving the boat and his brothers behind him.

Time ticked by, and the brothers soon lost their patience. Ignoring Maui's words, they leaped over to the new land and began trampling all across it, dividing it between them. But as they did so, the land thrashed underneath them, causing huge hills and jagged mountains to erupt from the surface, while other parts split into deep valleys or sunk into gloomy swamps.

Today the fish of Maui is better known as the North Island of New Zealand. And had Maui's brothers waited for him to return, perhaps it would be as flat and even as it had been, all those years ago.

Acknowledgements

Stories retold by: Sam Baer, Susanna Davidson,
Rosie Dickins and Rosie Hore
Edited by Lesley Sims and Susanna Davidson
Designed by Laura Nelson
Digital imaging by Nick Wakeford and Pete Taylor

First published in 2016 by Usborne Publishing Ltd., 83-85 Saffron Hill, London EC1N 8RT, England. www.usborne.com. Copyright © 2016 Usborne Publishing Limited. The name Usborne and the devices ♀☺ are Trade Marks of Usborne Publishing Ltd. All rights reserved. No part of this publication may be reproduced, stored in a retrieval system, or transmitted in any form or by any means, electronic, mechanical, photocopying, recording or otherwise, without the prior permission of the publisher. First published in America in 2016. UE.